ANDREW

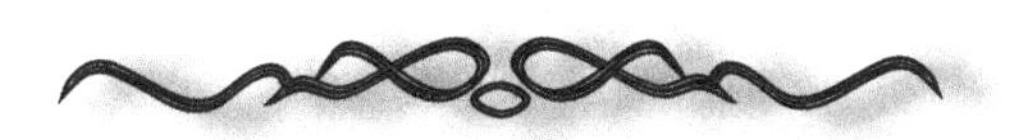

James Herman

Order this book online at **www.trafford.com**
or email orders@trafford.com

Most Trafford titles are also available at major online book retailers.

Printed in the United States of America.

ISBN: 978-1-4669-0662-4 (sc)
ISBN: 978-1-4669-0663-1 (hc)
ISBN: 978-1-4669-0661-7 (e)

Library of Congress Control Number: 2011961734

Trafford rev. 11/30/2011

North America & International
toll-free: 1 888 232 4444 (USA & Canada)
phone: 250 383 6864 • fax: 812 355 4082

Chapter One

WITHIN THE DEPTHS of the city, the flickering glow of a neon sign filtered down a desolate alley, illuminating a lone figure huddled in an alcove. Andrew, one of the many homeless despots and beggars often considered the cancer of society and cities across the nation, sat staring blankly into the semi-darkness, humming to himself.

The years on the street had not been kind to him. His face had the texture of leather, wrinkled by constant exposure to the elements. The tattered clothes he wore smelled from lack of personal hygiene. His long unkempt graying hair cascaded down the back of a tattered overcoat he was wearing. The stubble of a graying beard accentuated his bloodshot eyes giving him the appearance of a man much older than his actual age.

Clutched tightly in his hand was a brown paper bag, the shape of it resembling a bottle. Occasionally he would lift this to his mouth and take a swig.

He shivered as a gust of November wind penetrated his clothing, while stirring the lifeless refuse that managed to make its way into the alley. Repositioning himself, he glanced toward the main street, observing a couple passing and disappearing into the night.

Reaching into his shirt pocket, he withdrew a faded photo, faced it toward the dim light and gazed at it. The photo revealed a beautiful young teenage girl wearing a miniskirt. Her long blond hair cascading down to the small of her back was braided and adorned with beads.

He recalled how happy he was when the photo was taken. It was in the sixties. At the time, he felt he was on top of the world, and nobody or anything could upset his life. Never did he realize how wrong he could be. It was then he learned two important lessons in life. He came to realize it was not what people told you that could hurt you; it was what they did not tell you that really did the most harm. He learned how ones life could be changed unexpectedly by the whims of people you knew and unfortunately the ones you loved.

"Claire," he murmured as he looked at the photo.

Returning the picture to his coat pocket, he carefully listened to the street noises he was accustomed to hearing. Car horns blaring, people chattering and an occasional siren reached his ears. The music from the night club next door penetrated the surroundings and unknown doors along the alley opened and closed with loud bangs. The doors opening and closing was his main interest at the moment.

He could not recall how long he had been using the dead-end alley as a refuge. He felt secure in what he came to consider his private haven. Here, he assured himself, he would not be bothered by anyone, including the authorities.

A side door to the restaurant next to the alley opened. Someone tossed out two large trash bags, each landing with a loud thud on the pavement next to an overflowing trash container.

Andrew waited. The figure appeared several times more, each time relieving the inner room of its accumulated trash. This done, the door was closed and locked for the night. The sound of the dead bolt being latched was a signal for Andrew to make his move.

With difficulty, he stood up and staggered toward the trash bags, using the building walls to support him. Reaching the discarded bags, he sat on the cold pavement and set his brown paper bag on one of the steps leading to the door previously opened. A rat appeared, ran over his legs, and then scurried to parts unknown.

Pulling the bags toward him and opening them, a whiff of cooked food stuffs entered his nostrils. Though the contents of the bags were mixed as in a salad, he sifted through them in search of something to eat. This night the pickings were good.

Selecting from the discarded food, he retrieved portions of pork chops, baked potato, rare cooked steak and partially eaten pastries.

He ate until sated, then returned all he had not consumed back into the trash bags, removing evidence of any tampering. Assured all was in order, he picked up the brown paper bag and took a drink. Standing up, he started back to his resting place. On his way, he stopped to piss on a wall aiming the stream at a cockroach climbing the wall.

Although past midnight, Andrew did not go to sleep. He patiently waited for a signal to perform a nightly ritual he considered the most important event of the day. On schedule, a side door to the night club facing the alley opened. Several trash bags were thrown out, each making a loud clamor as they came to rest on the ground. When the door closed, he quickly made his way to these newly discarded treasures.

Reaching into a pocket of his overcoat, he withdrew a well used large plastic bag. Pulling one of the trash bags toward him, he opened it and began searching their contents.

Making two piles, he separated beer cans and liquor bottles. Having sorted the trash, he took one of the empty liquor bottles and set it aside, designating it a receptor. Carefully, he drained the meager contents of the other liquor bottles into the donor bottle. When he had finished, the selected bottle contained a mere swig of hard liquor, a prize hardly worth the effort. This, however, was Andrews's greatest joy, his dessert for the night as it was most nights.

He wiped the outside of the bottle with the sleeve of his coat, and then quickly put the bottle to his mouth letting the contents seep into his inner being. A warm sensation came over him as the mixture entered his body. What a delight he thought as he held the bottle for a few seconds being sure to capture all its contents.

Satisfied not a drop was to be spared, he cast away the bottle. As was his custom, he smashed the sorted beer cans with his foot to reduce the volume, and then placed them into the plastic bag. These, when traded for cash, along with other cans gathered earlier in the day would bring him enough cash to buy his necessary wine for the next day.

Completed with his nightly ritual and being sure everything appeared as though it had not been tampered with, he returned to his alcove.

As time passed, the night noises diminished, which became a time clock for Andrew. It was a signal for him to get some sleep, knowing this was the time of least activity by the authorities.

Even though being picked up and booked as a vagrant would be guaranteed food and a place to sleep for the night, he avoided this like the plague. He didn't enjoy spending the night in the city jail holding cell. It was the company he objected to and the harassment he often had to undergo. It also meant he would spend several days without any alcohol and the possible onset of the DT's. He learned to avoid the law no matter what the cost.

Retrieving a flattened cardboard box he kept hidden in an opening among a dilapidated brick wall, he placed it on the ground and sat down on it. Pushing his plastic bags containing the cans into a corner, he fashioned a pillow. Before lying down, he took another swig from the bottle. He shook the bottle to make sure there was still some wine left. This reserved wine would be his breakfast and hold him over until he could buy more. Making sure the cap to the bottle was tightly fastened; he placed it next to the bags, took off his overcoat and pulled it over himself, using it as a blanket. He laid down and fell asleep, not to stir until the next morning.

The loud clamor of trash cans hitting the pavement and noises from a garbage truck with its compacting mechanism in operation awakened Andrew from his sound sleep. Twice weekly these noises became his most prominent alarm clock. Other days, car horns, sirens, the screech of bus and truck brakes and strangers yelling or doors slamming would wake him.

Stirring but not getting up, he stared into the cold, steel gray sky. Looks as though it might rain, maybe snow he mused. Andrew smacked his lips. His mouth was dry and had a fowl taste. He sat up and as he did, the cold morning air penetrated his trousers. He had wet himself during his sleep, not an unusual occurrence. Undaunted by this mishap, he got up and donned the overcoat and returned the cardboard to its hiding place. Uncapping the wine bottle, he placed it to his mouth and drank until it was emptied. Tossing the bottle aside, he picked up his bags of cans and swiftly walked out of the alley into the busy street.

Andrew kept from making direct eye contact with people approaching him from the opposite direction. Inwardly, he was not proud of his condition, but assured himself he could not do anything about his situation. He did not want to get into any confrontation with anyone and felt the lack of eye contact was the best way to prevent confrontations.

He traveled the same three blocks as he had done so many times in the past, crossed over railroad tracks, paralleled them for another five blocks, then stopped at the gates in front of a scrap yard. A sign over the gates announced "MARTY'S RECYCLING PLANT"

A smaller sign hung next to the gates. It indicated the buying of copper, brass, aluminum cans, scrap metal of all sorts, and also the current various purchasing prices. He noted that aluminum cans had risen to fifty-four cents a pound. He held up his bags, judging their weight. Sixteen pounds, he imagined.

Throwing the bags over his back, he walked into the scrap yard and headed toward a shack housing the cashier. Reaching it, he waited for the customer ahead of him to complete his transaction. When finished, Andrew stepped up to the service window. The young woman he was accustomed to seeing was not at the window. Instead, a short, rotund balding man with a scarred but jovial face stood at the window.

Andrew felt apprehensive as he noticed the attendant appeared to be studying him. He shifted nervously as the man pondered him.

"Do I know you?" the attendant queried.

"I don't think so," Andrew replied.

"Have you been here before?"

"Yes sir."

"What's in those bags?"

"Aluminum cans."

"Alright, put your bags on the scale platform and step back away from it."

Andrew carefully set the bags down on a large platform scale adjacent to the customers' window. The attendant stepped outside the shack and with a noticeable limp, walked up to where Andrew was standing. Andrew fidgeted, as the attendant began to study him once again. After the short pause he spoke.

"Let's see what you have," he finally said, as he pushed one of several buttons on the scale.

Andrew waited in anticipation.

"That'll be . . . eight dollars and sixty-four cents," he announced after the scale made its calculations from the weight placed on it. "But I'll have to take off for the weight of the bags."

Andrew didn't say anything, knowing the bags weighed only a few ounces. He was not about to get into an argument with the attendant.

"Dump those cans in one of those wheeled plastic containers over there," the attendant said, pointing toward the containers. He returned to the weigh shack, reappearing at the customers' window and waited for Andrew to dump his cans.

"Look here!" the attendant yelled, while shaking his finger at Andrew. "I saw some water coming out of those cans when you dumped them so I'll have to deduct off your total weight."

Andrew returned to the window but didn't respond even though he was careful to empty the cans as he gathered them.

"Here's your money," the attendant said.

Andrew extended his hand to receive his money. He paused with his hand still outstretched after receiving a five dollar bill.

"Well? What are you waiting for? Go! Get out of here. I've got things to do," the attendant said in a gruff voice.

Andrew clasped the bill in his hand, turned around, then headed toward the gates he had previously entered. He had become accustomed to this type of treatment, but learned to leave well enough alone. Confrontations in the past only caused him unwanted trouble. He stopped at the gates, removed one of his shoes and placed the bill in it. As he was putting his shoe back on, he was suddenly startled by an outcry coming from the shack.

"Hey! You! Come back here," the attendant called out.

The sudden outcry startled Andrew. Expecting trouble from the outburst, his instinct was to run, but he thought otherwise. In running, he feared the attendant might call the police, claiming he had stolen the five dollars. He reluctantly turned around and with caution returned to the service window.

Once again, the attendant studied Andrew intently.

"I have a strange feeling I know you, but I can't place where or when we could have met," the attendant finally commented after a few minutes. "Time will tell. Anyway, I'm short handed today and I was wondering if you know where the deli on Forth Street is located."

Andrew nodded.

"Good!" the attendant exclaimed. "I know it's a bit early for lunch, but if you'll go there for me and get some sandwiches, I'll buy you lunch and give you a few bucks for your trouble. It looks as though you could use something to eat. How about it?"

"Yes sir," Andrew replied.

"Great!" The attendant replied. He opened the cash register and took out seven dollars. "Here's seven bucks. Get us each a Rueben sandwich. With tax it will come to three fifteen each, so that'll be six thirty total. Make sure you bring back the correct change."

Andrew took the money, carefully folded the bills and put them into the pocket of his overcoat. He turned and quickly walked to the gates, passed beneath them and into the busy street. As he continued onward, it began to sleet.

He flipped the collar of the overcoat up around his neck in an attempt to keep the sleet from hitting the back of his neck, all the while keeping his head down.

Just as he was about to cross over the railroad tracks, a locomotive switch engine with several box cars attached came swiftly down the tracks he was about to cross over. The whistle of the locomotive gave out a loud shrill, announcing its presence. Andrew jumped back, realizing he was about to be run over. As he did, due to the accumulation of sleet, he lost his footing and fell. His knee came down hard on the edge of a cross tie. Down he went, landing in a puddle of mud several feet from the tracks.

He laid there for a moment, as the pain in his knee seemed to reach every nerve in his body. It was several minutes before the pain eased and he was over the shock of the fall. He picked himself up, making an attempt to brush off the mud that had managed to cling to his clothes. It was fruitless, as the attempt only made matters worse.

Now limping, he walked as fast as he could toward Forth Street. Although he kept close to the buildings using them as a shield against the unrelenting sleet, his coat and clothes became soaked. He was one block away from the deli when he noticed an all too familiar sign. The sign announced, "HOLIDAY LIQUOR STORE"

Andrew stepped into a vestibule of an adjacent store. He became jittery while staring at the sign knowing what he wanted to do. He put his hand to his mouth and brushed his whiskers as though in deep thought, keeping his eyes on the sign.

Putting his hand into the coat pocket, he fondled the folded bills that attendant had given him. Withdrawing his hand, he stooped down, untied his shoe and retrieved the five dollar bill he had received from his can sale. He carefully counted the money. Twelve dollars, he counted. He could not remember when he had that much money all at one time.

The urge to cross the street and enter the liquor store became his foremost thought. Usually by this time of the morning, he had already secured his alcohol for the day. He was about to walk toward the store, but the thought of the attendant came to mind. He began to wonder what the attendant might do if he didn't return to the scrap yard.

Fearful the attendant might cause him some unwanted trouble, and realizing he could not ever return to the scrap yard to sell his cans, he decided it best to hold off on getting any wine for the moment. He reasoned with the additional money the attendant promised for getting the sandwiches, he would have more money to spend, enough to buy his supply of booze to last him several days. He assured himself he would have plenty of time after he finished the chore for the attendant.

Andrew stepped out of the vestibule and walked to the deli. Upon reaching it, he opened the door and quickly stepped inside, noticing the store was void of customers, the only person beside himself being the counter man. The heavy-set pot bellied counter man, wearing a slightly stained apron looked up as Andrew entered.

"Hey you?" he called out as Andrew closed the door. "We don't give out freebies to the likes of you, so just turn around and get out of here."

Andrew was startled at the sudden attack. "I have money," he said in defense.

The counter man looked him over a moment. "Alright, but make it quick. I don't want you around when my regular customers come in to get their lunch, and you need to take your order with you, not eat it here. Got that? Now what do you want?"

"Two Reuben sandwiches," Andrew replied.

"Two Rueben sandwiches," the man mocked as Andrew drew closer to the counter. "Let me see the money first."

Andrew took the folded bills out of his pocket and showed the money to him. Appearing satisfied, the short order cook turned around and busied himself preparing the sandwiches. When finished, he placed them in Styrofoam containers and set them on the counter.

"That'll be eight bucks."

"Eight dollars!" Andrew exclaimed.

"Yeah, eight plus tax since it's a take-out order."

Andrew looked up at the menu over the counter. "Your sign says three fifteen each, tax included."

"Oh! So you can read? Well I don't care what the sign reads. Its eight bucks plus I have to charge you for the Styrofoam containers. These sandwiches are already made so you've got to pay for them."

Andrew's face flushed. He was about to say something when suddenly the counter man picked up a cleaver and pointed it toward him.

"Look you! Put the money on the counter, take your sandwiches and get the hell out of here or I'll call the cops."

Andrew held his voice. He placed two five dollar bills on the counter. The counter man picked up the bills, opened the cash register, placing them in their respective compartment. He closed the drawer.

Andrew waited, expecting his change.

"Go! Get out of here," the counter man yelled.

Andrew picked up the sandwiches, turned and headed for the door. Reaching it, he opened it and stepped outside. As he was closing the door behind himself, the counter man laughed loudly.

Realizing there was nothing he could do about the overcharge, Andrew slowly walked back to the scrap yard. He could not contain his anger and began swearing. Two women dressed in business attire approaching him, looked at him with disgust.

"What a disgraceful drunken bum," one said as they passed him.

Resenting the slur, Andrew stopped, turned around and yelled. "I'm not a drunken bum!"

The two laughed as they continued on their way. This infuriated Andrew even more. About to pass a building, he stopped and peered inside to catch sight of the clock in the lobby. It read eleven thirty.

Noticing the time, Andrew forgot his anger. It should have only taken him about an hour to complete the chore. What would the attendant say? How would he be able to explain being overcharged for the sandwiches? He walked in silence, all the while worried as to the attendants' reaction to his lengthy delay when he returned to the scrap yard.

"What took you so long?" the attendant growled as Andrew reached the service window.

"Sleet," Andrew quickly replied, hoping the attendant would be satisfied.

He eyed Andrews' now-drenched clothing. "Well, you did come back, so that's worth something. Okay, come inside," the attendant said. "Go around to the side door, and I'll let you in."

Andrew quickly walked to the side door and waited patiently. The attendant unlocked the door and opened it. Andrew stepped inside.

"Go stand by that stove," the attendant said, pointing to a pot bellied stove in the center of the room, as he closed the door and locked it.

"Did you get the sandwiches like I asked?" he said as he limped toward Andrew.

"Yes sir!" he replied, withdrawing the two Styrofoam containers from under his overcoat.

"My change?" the attendant queried with raised eyebrows.

Andrew lowered his head. He reached into his pocket and took out the remaining two dollars and handed them to the attendant.

"This is all I have left," he said.

"That's too much. You only owe me seventy cents. You do know how to count change, don't you?'

"Yes, but the man at the counter didn't give me any change back when I handed him two five dollar bills."

"What?"

"Yes sir. He said the sandwiches were four dollars apiece plus a charge for the containers and tax."

"Damn it!" the attendant muttered as he handed Andrew one of the containers. He gave the two dollars back to him.

"You stay put and eat. I'll take care of this matter."

The attendant returned to the service window and sat down on a stool. He opened the container, removed the sandwich and took a quick bite. He picked up the phone and dialed a number and began speaking in a low voice. Finishing his phone call, he opened the cash register, withdrew three dollar bills, and then returned to Andrew.

"I talked with the owner of the deli, whom I know personally. He's going to take care of the overcharge for me, so don't worry about my change. Here's your money he overcharged you."

"Thank you," Andrew said sheepishly.

The attendant returned to the service window and continued eating his sandwich. He watched Andrew, pondering him. He didn't know what to make of him, but noticed he was polite and he did do what was asked of him. There was still a daunting thought he knew Andrew, which plagued him.

Andrew became uneasy as the attendant continued peering at him. After pondering Andrew for several minutes, he got up off the stool and returned to where Andrew was standing.

"Look, I need someone to do some work for me around this place. How about you? It looks as though you could use some work. The guy I had working for me didn't show up again, in fact he hasn't been around for the past few days. Tell you what, if you're willing to work for me, I'll give you three bucks an hour and I'll throw in lunch. How about it?"

Andrew was taken aback at the offer. He had long ago given up looking for menial work. Even temporary services wouldn't hire him. He felt he was not an ideal employee. No one, he assured himself, wanted to hire a street walker, a bum. Over the shock of the attendants query, Andrew, for the first time since he could recall, looked the attendant in eye. "Yes sir, if you have a mind to use me," he replied.

"Good!" The attendant smiled, "But I can't have you working around here with what you're wearing. We'll have to do something about those clothes you have on."

The attendant limped to some cabinets at the rear of the shack and began to open and close various cabinet doors. The noises of the doors resounded throughout the shack as the attendant appeared to be searching for something. Finished with his search, he returned to Andrew with an armful of clothes.

"Here! Take off those old rags you're wearing and put these on," he said as he handed them to Andrew. "They're not new, but clean and much better than what you've got on now. You can change in the toilet room in the back."

The attendant pointed toward a door in the rear of the room.

Andrew took the clothes, went into the toilet room, closing the door behind himself.

Andrew wasted little time changing, donning a pair of dungaree pants and chambray shirt, apparent discards from a former sailor. Finished changing clothes, he opened the door and stepped back into the shacks proper. The attendant had his back turned toward him, as he spoke to a customer at the service window. After he finished the transaction, the attendant turned his attention toward Andrew.

"That's much better," he said, while giving Andrew the once over. "Yes much better, but we'll have to do something about that scruffy beard of yours. I'll get you some things you can use to clean up and shave later, and you'll have to put your hair into a pony tail so you don't get it caught in any equipment around here."

The attendant walked over to the side door and opened it.

"You can throw those old clothes you were wearing away. In fact, throw them in that burn barrel I fired up," he said.

Andrew was about to do as the attendant asked when he suddenly stopped him.

"Hold on a minute. What's your name?" he asked.

"Simpson," Andrew answered.

"Andrew Simpson?" the attendant quizzed to be sure he heard him correctly.

"Yes. Andrew Simpson," he replied, surprised the attendant mentioned his first name.

"Andrew Simpson!" exclaimed the attendant. "I use to know an Andrew Simpson, years ago. Could you be that Andrew Simpson?"

Andrew studied the man standing before him. He searched his mind trying to recall if he had ever met anybody with a scarred face and walking with a limp.

"No sir," Andrew replied, after searching his memory. "I don't recall ever meeting anyone like you."

The attendant put his hand to his chin and mussed. "I suppose you could be right. Simpson is a common name and it being a large metropolitan city, there could be several Andrew Simpson's around. Well anyway, my name is Marty Fieldman. You can call me Marty," he said, pausing, waiting for some sort of acknowledgement on Andrew's face that would indicate he knew him. There was no change in his expression.

Andrew noticed disappointment on Marty's face.

"Okay, then," he said. "I'm the owner, operator and chief bottle washer of this scrap yard. Tell you what, you give me a good days' work and I might have a mind to keep you on. That is, if you have a mind to stay. The man working before you arrived is finished as far as I'm concerned. He never was very reliable and after all the good I did for him. Go on now, get rid of those old clothes like I told you, and come back in here so I can tell you what it is I expect of you."

Andrew walked out the side door and located the burn barrel. Retrieving his cherished photo and money, he threw his old clothes into the fire while holding onto his overcoat. The fire flared up from the new fuel. Marty watched from the service window. Opening the window, he shouted. "Hey! Throw that coat into the fire. It's worse than those clothes you were wearing."

Andrew quickly threw the overcoat into the barrel. Once again the fire flared.

Marty called out once again. "Go into that metal building just to your left. Inside you'll find a Pea coat hanging on a nail. Put it on and come back here."

Andrew did as Marty had instructed. Finding the Pea coat inside the metal building, he donned it, and returned to the shack. As he stepped inside the door, Marty tossed a watch cap at him. Andrew tried to catch it, but missed, dropping the money and photo he was holding. He reached down and picked the cap, money and photo.

"What's that?" Marty questioned, noticing the photo.

Andrew attempted to hide it. It was his prize possession, his only link to times past.

"Just a picture," Andrew replied.

Marty walked over to him and took the photo. His eyes widened as he studied the picture. Andrew noticed the surprise look on his face.

"Where did you get this?" Marty demanded.

"It's mine," Andrew replied, in defense as though being accused of a crime.

"Who's the girl?" Marty asked in anticipation.

"It was a girl I knew a long time ago," Andrew replied.

Marty appeared puzzled. "This is a picture of Claire Maxwell. How is it you have a picture of her?"

Andrew became disturbed. "She was my wife?"

"What?" Marty gasped.

Andrew stepped back.

"It is you. I thought so. You're Andrew Simpson, the Andrew Simpson I use to know long ago. I'm Marty. Don't you remember me?"

Andrew shook his head, still not recalling.

"You were my brother-in-law. I was married to Elizabeth Maxwell, Claire's sister," Marty said cautiously.

"You couldn't have been married to Elizabeth," Andrew quickly replied. "She was married to a Martin, huh? I don't recall his last name but do remember his first name was Martin, not Marty."

Marty gave a sigh of relief. "Of course, how forgetful I am. I'm Martin, or was Martin Phelpman. I changed my name long ago. When . . . when it happened."

Andrew lowered his head as he recalled what happened to Elizabeth. He didn't realize the outcome of the event left Marty severely disfigured and lame, the reason he didn't recognize him.

Marty grabbed his hand and patted it, then gave him a big hug. Andrew did not know how to react.

Marty broke away from the embrace. He patted Andrew on the shoulder. "It is good to see you Andrew," he said. Marty beaming as though meeting a long lost relative.

"Stay here and work for me," he pleaded. "A lot has happened since we last knew each other. Will you stay?"

"Yes," Andrew replied, although he felt somewhat elated at the chance meeting with his ex brother-in-law, he was apprehensive, not really sure of Martys' motives.

"Good!" Marty said. "However, there's one thing I insist on while you're working for me. No booze."

From the appearance he presented earlier, Marty knew what kind of life Andrew was living. It saddened him realizing he was not the Andrew he had once known and that he had degraded to such a state.

Andrew felt uncomfortable as Marty sized him up. He looked down at the floor. He sensed Marty had figured out what was taking place in his life.

"Yes sir," Andrew reluctantly replied, while staring at the floor. Inwardly he felt he would be able to work with Marty, although he questioned his ability to keep off the liquor while working. He decided he would cross that bridge when he came to it.

A bell rang, resounding throughout the weigh shack. Marty turned toward the service window as the ring announced the presence of a new costumer.

"Wait here," he said, as he turned to accommodate the client.

When finished a few minutes later, Marty returned to Andrew. He was in deep thought, wondering why Marty was suddenly taking an interest in him, especially in his condition.

"Don't think about it," Marty said as if reading his thoughts. "It looks as though you need help and I'm here to give it to you. Besides there is something you need to, huh . . . ," Marty stopped short of what he had on his mind.

Andrew looked at him curiously, wondering what he was about to say.

CHAPTER TWO

THEIR INTERACTION WAS cut short by the sound of a buzzer ringing inside the shack. Marty walked to the service window and called out.

"Andrew, I need you up here."

Andrew quickly put the photo and money back into his shirt pocket and walked to where Marty was standing.

"Go with this man and unload his truck," Marty said. "I'll be down in a few minutes and show you what to do."

"Yes sir," Andrew acknowledged as he quickly donned the watch cap and stepped outside.

When he drew near the truck, the owner, wearing a leather jacket and gloves motioned for him to get inside the cab. Andrew climbed into the cab and waited. After a few moments the driver joined him. As the heater in the cab circulated the warm air, the smell from Andrew's unwashed body began to permeate the inside of the trucks' cab.

The driver was about to put the truck into gear, when he suddenly paused and turned toward Andrew. He brushed at his well-groomed goatee with his hand.

"You stink. Don't you ever take a bath?"

Andrew's face reddened in embarrassment. It has been years since he took a bath or even considered taking one. So accustomed he had become to his own smell, it did not bother him, nor did he realize or care how offensive it had become to those he encountered.

The truck moved slowly down the road among the masses of scrap, finally stopping at a machine used for blowing aluminum cans into a trailer. The driver maneuvered his truck into position, stopped and waited.

"This is where you get out," the driver said without glancing at Andrew.

Andrew quickly departed the cab and stood outside waiting for Marty to arrive. Several minutes passed before Marty appeared, approaching the truck.

As Marty neared the truck, he called toward Andrew, motioning as he spoke, "Get up on the back of the truck and throw down some of those sacks."

The truck was loaded to the hilt with bags of aluminum cans. Andrew climbed up one side of the truck, folded back the tarp covering the load, grabbed two sacks and tossed them down toward Marty.

"Good," Marty said. "Jump down here so I can show you what to do."

Andrew jumped down off the truck as Marty picked up the two bags, and walked to a metal platform a few feet away, setting the bags on it.

"This platform is an automatic scale," Marty said. "It weighs anything that's placed on it. All you have to do is push the button that corresponds to the type of metal you're weighing. In this case, since we're weighing aluminum cans, push this button, the one marked *aluminum*."

Andrew watched as Marty pushed the button.

"When you've done that, put the cans into this hopper and press this button. Make sure you put only cans not the bags with the cans into the hopper. The hopper feeds a short conveyor belt that feeds the cans into another hopper with a strong magnet at its end, to catch non-aluminum cans. That hopper has high-powered fans that blow the cans into the trailer."

Marty went through the procedure, making sure Andrew saw every move he made.

When Marty was finished with has demonstration, he made Andrew do the same. After going through the procedure several times with Andrew and assuring him he was doing the job correctly, Marty left Andrew alone with his task and returned to the weight shack.

Andrew quickly set about unloading the truck, weighing the sacks, putting the cans into the hopper, and blowing them into the trailer, as Marty had instructed. The temperature, though dropping by the minute, did not bother him, as he was generating his own heat from his work. He was not mindful of the time and how quickly it was passing. It was several hours before the last sack of cans was weighed and blown into the trailer.

Done with the unloading and weighing, Andrew walked to the driver's side of the truck. The driver was fast asleep inside the warm cab. He banged on the door with his fist. The driver stirred and opened his eyes. He looked at Andrew and rolled down the window.

"Yeah?" he asked, sounding irritated.

"All the sacks have been weighed," Andrew replied.

"Good," the driver said. He rolled up the window, put the truck in gear and drove off, leaving Andrew behind.

Andrew stood with a blank look on his face, not expecting to be left standing out in the cold. He was surprised by the driver's action, but then recalled the comment about his smell. He shrugged his shoulders, put the collar of his pea coat up around his neck and headed for the weigh shack.

As Andrew walked on, huge mounds of scrap material of various types came into view. He was amazed at the volume of material. *How can people be so wasteful,* he wondered, *when there are so many in need?* The thought plagued his mind as he continued onward. Several minutes later, he reached the weigh sack.

"You finally made it," Marty commented, as Andrew closed the door. "You did well down there. In fact, better than I expected."

"Thank you," Andrew replied.

Marty pondered a moment. "Well, time to close up shop for today," he said, then turned toward the cash register, opened it and withdrew some money, counting it as he did.

"Here you go," he said, handing Andrew several bills.

Andrew took the money and stuffed it into his coat pocket without bothering to count it.

"There's twenty-four dollars there," Marty said, noticing that Andrew had not counted the money. "It's your wages for the day. Now, what I want you to do is go somewhere and wash up, take a bath, a shower, or something. I don't want any of my workers being offensive to my customers."

"Yes, sir," Andrew replied, his face flushing at Martys' comment.

"Be here tomorrow at eight on the dot. Okay?"

Andrew nodded.

"Be off with you, then. I'll see you in the morning."

Andrew departed the shack and began walking toward the gates when Marty suddenly called out "Hold on a moment."

Andrew stopped, turned around, and waited to see what Marty wanted. After a few seconds, Marty tossed a plastic sack toward him. It landed on the ground close to Andrew. He picked up the bag and glanced inside it. Marty had placed several toiletry items in it.

"There are some things you might need," Marty said, before closing the service window.

Andrew wanted to thank him, but saw it would be useless, as Marty would not be able to hear him. Andrew turned around and headed back to the streets. He kept his hands in the pockets of the pea coat, fondling the money he had just received.

Not having had any alcohol since earlier in the morning, his first priority was to get some as soon as possible. It was already past five. He feared the liquor store might be closed by the time he got to it. As quickly as he could, he headed to Forth Street, to the very liquor store he'd passed earlier in the day.

When he reached the store, much to his dismay, it was closed. He cursed beneath his breath. He left the store and walked to First Street where another liquor store was located. That store was also closed when he reached it. He peered into the store's interior, hoping someone might be inside. There was no one. He became alarmed knowing he would have to spend the night deprived of alcohol. Other liquor stores at a much further distance, he knew, would also be closed for the day.

As he stood at the entrance, he recalled what Marty had told him, which became a battle with his desire for alcohol. He lowered his head, realizing he had to make a decision about his drinking. Would it be the booze, sleeping on the streets, and a life of misery, or an honest attempt to better himself? His fate was in his hands.

His thoughts were soon interrupted, when a bright light was trained on him. A police car had pulled up in front of the liquor store.

"You there," a voice rang out from within the car. "What are your doing?"

Andrew turned toward the light. He put his hand up, shielding the glare from the light. It was no use. He could not see the occupants of the car, with the light blinding him against the darkness.

"Put both hands behind your head," the voice bellowed.

Apprehensive, Andrew quickly put his hands behind his head. He had been through this before, and he dreaded what was about to happen.

One of the car doors slammed. Andrew stood motionless. He could almost hear his heart pounding.

As Andrew expected, the figure of a uniformed police officer appeared. The officer had his revolver drawn. The din from the police radio blaring echoed throughout the surrounding area.

"Turn around and put your hands against the wall," the officer said, as he approached Andrew.

Andrew turned and put his hands against the wall and spread his legs.

"Oh! So you've been through this before?" the police officer said sarcastically, noticing Andrew automatically spread his legs without being to do so.

Andrew did not say a word. The officer frisked him and when assured he was not carrying a concealed weapon, put his gun back into its holster, while telling Andrew to put his hands down.

"Okay, mister. What are you doing here?"

Andrew thought quickly. He knew if his answer was not right, he could spend the night in jail.

"Ah . . . I was supposed to meet a friend here," he quickly replied. "I think I may have missed him."

The officer contemplated the clothes Andrew was wearing "You don't look like a vagrant," he said. "From those clothes you are wearing, I suppose you are off one of those ships down at the docks. Are you?"

"Yes sir," replied Andrew, thankful for the clothes Marty had given him. At his reply the spotlight went dim.

"It looks like you missed your friend," the officer said.

"I guess so," Andrew replied.

"Where are you staying?"

"Oh, I was going to get a room at the YMCA," Andrew quickly replied, hoping the officer would be satisfied.

"Good, then we'll give you a lift."

"No need officer. I can walk," Andrew said.

"No. We insist," the officer said, with a voice that was more demanding than before. "Being just off a ship and your pockets full of money, you don't know what you might run into on these streets. We wouldn't want you getting robbed."

"No, I guess not," Andrew said as he walked to the car. The officer opened the rear door for him.

"He's clean. Just a sailor off one of the ships at the docks," the officer said to his partner as he got in the police cruiser.

As the car started to move, the police officer picked up the radio and informed the dispatcher that his unit was taking someone to the YMCA.

"Thank goodness," Andrew thought.

The trip was short. When the police cruiser pulled in front of the YMCA, one of the officers got out of the car and opened the door for Andrew as there were no door handles on the inside rear doors.

"You have a good evening sailor," he said, as Andrew got out of the police cruiser.

"Thank you officer," Andrew replied.

"No trouble!"

Andrew paused, not sure what his next move would be. He expected the policeman to get into the cruiser and move on, but when the officer got back into the car, it did not move.

Due to Andrew pausing, the officer on the passengers' side of the squad car rolled down the window. "Is there a problem?" he asked.

"No sir," Andrew responded, then turned and slowly walked to the doors. He opened the lobby door, glancing back to see if the police cruiser had departed. It had not. Andrew stepped into the lobby, letting the door close behind him. He glanced around, feeling apprehensive as to what he should do.

A clerk behind the registration counter greeted him.

"Good evening sailor. May I help you?"

"Ah . . . evening," Andrew replied

"Do you need a room for the night sir?" the clerk inquired as he give Andrew the once over.

Andrew smiled at the clerk. It was the second time he had been mistaken for a sailor.

"How much does a room cost?"

"A private room with a community bath room at end of the hallway is fifteen for the night."

Andrew was taken aback at the cost. He did not realize how devalued the dollar had become since dropping out of society. Feeling awkward, Andrew put his hand into his pocket and again fondled his money. He knew he had enough for the private room, but did not want to spend that much, preferring to save his money for his wine.

The clerk, realizing Andrew was uncomfortable, quickly intoned. "We do have a dormitory with bunk beds and a community shower for five dollars, if you prefer," the clerk volunteered.

"I'll take a bunk," Andrew quickly replied.

The clerk reached under the counter, withdrew a post card sized form, made a notation on it, and handed it to Andrew along with a pen.

"Please fill this card out," he said.

Andrew took the card and looked at it, pausing. He did not know what to do with it. It had been many years since he had been required to write or fill out any form or document.

The clerk waited patiently, watching Andrew's every move. Noticing the expression of uncertainty on his face and not wanting to add to his discomfort, the clerk reached for the card.

"Here, let me help you. Those things can be a pain."

Andrew handed the card back to the clerk. The clerk set about filling out the form. Having written in Andrews' name after receiving this information from him, without looking up he asked. "Address?"

Andrews face flushed. He did not know what to reply. The clerk, while still not looking up, made an entry on the form. He continued writing until the card was completed. It was apparent that the clerk was familiar with prospective tenants such as Andrew. He handed the card back to him.

"Please sign your name on the line I marked with an X," the clerk instructed.

Andrew took the card and pen. In a grade school penmanship manner, he carefully signed his name on the form, and then handed the card back to the clerk. Without giving it a thought, not looking at the form, the clerk put the card in a file box on the counter.

"That'll be five dollars in advance please."

Andrew reached into his pocket and withdrew his money. He unraveled the crumbed bills, selected the proper amount and handed the cash to the clerk. The clerk took the money and put it in the cash register. He was about to give Andrew a receipt, but crumbled the receipt and threw it into the trash can. Turning toward a board with numbers on it, the clerk mused. Gathering information known only to him, the clerk turned back to Andrew.

"The dormitory is on the fifth floor. It has some empty bunks. You can take the elevator."

Andrew walked to the elevator lobby. One of the elevator doors opened as he approached it. He stepped inside and pressed the 5 button.

Within a few minutes, the elevator door opened to the lobby of the fifth floor. Andrew stepped out of the car and looked around. He noticed a large sign above double doors adjacent to the elevator.

Men's dormitory! The sign indicated.

Beside the doors was a smaller sign displaying the rules expected of the residents staying in the dormitory. After carefully reading all the rules, he opened one of the double doors and stepped inside. Pausing, he waited for his eyes to become accustomed to the darkness. The din from the unseen men snoring, coughing, moaning, tossing and turning echoed throughout the room. While waiting, he pondered the unseen occupants. How many of these men are just like me he wondered.

Slowly he could see, by way of the many exit lights, the layout of the dormitory. Careful not to disturb anyone, he made his way through the maze of bunk beds, finally reaching an empty one.

He put his hand on the bunk, feeling the softness of the mattress. He felt the pillow, bent down and smelled it. He could not remember when last he had slept in a bed with clean sheets, a pillow and a blanket to cover with. A feeling of comfort came over him. For the first time since he could remember he felt happy.

Andrew removed his money from his pea coat pocket and put it in his pants pocket. Taking off the watch cap, he placed it in the pea coat pocket, and then carefully laid the coat and plastic bag Marty had given him over the metal frame at the head of the bed. After removing his shoes, he placed them under the bunk. Without taking off his clothes, he slid beneath the covers, falling fast asleep.

It seemed but a few minutes, when suddenly the lights in the dormitory came on. Startled by the sudden brightness, Andrew quickly sat up in the bunk.

An unknown voice announced. "Time gentlemen!"

Andrew continued sitting and waited until he was fully awake. He looked around and watched as his fellow occupants went about the task of getting ready for the days events. He pondered his situation. Realizing he liked this environment, compared to that of sleeping in an alley, he vowed he would do his best to take advantage of his new found opportunity since his small income would allow such luxury.

Fully awake, Andrew recalled the comment made about his smell the previous day. Realizing he had to do something about his personal hygiene, he watched as some of the men wrapped in towels headed toward a door marked showers. He knew he had best do the same.

He waited until the population of the dormitory thinned out. Assured he would not be an embarrassment to himself, he picked up his coat and plastic bag and went to the shower room, opened the door and stepped inside looking around as he did. He was pleased he had waited as the shower area had emptied of occupants. Scattered about the room, lying on shower benches, over toilet stall door and on various sinks, were used towels and washcloths. A sigh caught Andrews's eyes.

TOWEL AND WASHCLOTH RENTAL $1.00.

Not wanting to spend his precious money, he searched each of the discarded towels. Finally he selected one that seemed the least soiled. He picked it up, grabbed a used washcloth, and then headed for the shower stalls.

Grateful no one was around; Andrew undressed and placed his clothes on the bench just outside the shower stall. Naked, he searched each stall until he came to one with a partial bar of soap left behind by a previous user. Stepping inside the stall and closing the canvas curtain, he turned on the water and soon was lost in the task of showering. The warm water flowed over his body. He so enjoyed the comfort of the shower, he was not aware three quarters of an hour had passed.

Suddenly someone announced. "You only have half an hour to vacate mister."

"I'm almost finished," Andrew called out as he turned off the water.

He parted the canvas curtain and stepped out of the shower stall, making his way through the mist created by the water vapors to the bench where he had placed his clothes. He dried off and quickly dressed. When finished, he walked to one of the many sinks in the connecting shower room. Reaching a sink, he looked into the mirror above it. He stared at his reflection pondering the view before him. He was saddened at what he saw.

Through abuse, alcohol and weathering, a tired, haggard face stared back at him. He realized he could do nothing about the past, but felt comfort knowing the future could be different. He pondered the growth of beard on his face.

He opened the plastic bag given to him by Marty. Reaching inside, he withdrew a razor, a tube of toothpaste, toothbrush and comb. He turned on the water and placed a discarded piece of soap under it, working the bar into lather. Placing the later on his face, with difficulty he shaved off the beard. Satisfied with the results, he returned to the bench, and reached down to get his shoes. To his surprise, they were not where he thought he had put them before showering. They were nowhere to be found. Thinking he might have left them at the bunk, Andrew quickly walked back into the dormitory.

Janitors were busy removing sheets and remaking the bunks for the next night's occupants. Andrew reached the bunk he had slept in. He looked under it but could not find his shoes. As he continued searching, one of the janitors noticed him.

"May I help you?"

"My shoes," he replied. "Have you seen any shoes under this bunk?"

"No sir," the janitor said, as he continued with his job, seeming not to care as to Andrews' plight.

With disgust, Andrew turned around and walked out of the dormitory. He knew he could not go out in the street without shoes. He stepped into an elevator and pushed the lobby button. After reaching the lobby, he quickly walked to the registration desk. A different clerk was at the desk when he had reached it.

"Good morning sailor," the clerk said with a smile.

"Good morning," Andrew replied.

"May I help you?" the clerk asked, noticing Andrew was not wearing any shoes.

"My shoes!" Andrew blurted. "They're gone."

The clerk appeared somewhat sympathetic, but was at a loss as to what to say. Seeing Andrew had no luggage, he inquired. "I suppose your clothing is aboard ship?"

"Ah . . . Yes," Andrew replied.

The clerk pondered the situation for a few moments. "Why don't you go into that room next to the elevator lobby," he suggested. "The room with the USO signs on the door. Maybe they can help you."

"Thank you," Andrew said, as he quickly turned and walked to the door with the USO sign on it.

Opening the door, he stepped inside. Except for two women behind a table, the room was vacant. A coffee urn and some doughnuts on a paper plate, rested on the table.

One of the two volunteers asked. "May we help you?"

Andrew didn't say anything. He walked toward the table. When he got closer, the volunteer commented. "Oh! You must be a merchant marine."

"My shoes! They're gone. I stayed here last night. Someone took my shoes."

The two volunteers bent over the table to see his plight.

"My my!" One of the matronly women mused. "Well, don't worry, I may know someone who can help you," she added, as she picked up the phone receiver on the table.

He stood by the table as the USO volunteer dialed a number. When she began speaking, she turned her back to Andrew. After several moments, the volunteer put the receiver back in the cradle.

"There will be someone here to help you shortly. Would you like some coffee and a doughnut while you wait? There is no charge."

"Yes. Thank you," Andrew replied.

Andrew helped himself to the meager breakfast. Feeling somewhat sheepish, he walked across the room and sat down on one of the folding chairs set up for perspective visitors. A half hour passed. He started to get nervous when he noticed the two ladies behind the table occasionally glanced at him.

Another fifteen minutes passed, when one of the doors opened. A man carrying a plastic bag stepped inside and walked up to the two volunteers. After a few words, one of the volunteers pointed in the direction of Andrew. The man turned and walked toward him. As he approached, Andrew could see that the man was wearing a Salvation Army uniform.

"I see you're without shoes," the man said.

"Yes sir. Someone took them."

"Well, I'm here to help," he said. Opening the bag, the man withdrew several pairs of slightly used work shoes. "Here, try these on and see if any fit."

Andrew tried on several shoes, finally selecting a pair that fit best.

"These feel good," Andrew commented.

"Good! Then they're yours now."

"How much do I own you?" Andrew asked.

"Nothing at all," the man said. He turned around and departed the room.

Andrew thanked the volunteers, walked out of the room, through the lobby, then out into the street.

It was dawn. People were going about their daily task of getting to work. No one seemed to notice him which pleased him. Realizing it was too early to be at the scrap yard, he walked slowly, attempting to pass as much time as possible. As he walked, to his dismay, his hands began to tremble.

The desire for alcohol became strong. It was too early for any of the liquor store to be open.

Andrew was perplexed. He needed to get some alcohol and quick. Suddenly, Chancy, a long time friend came to mind. He knew Chancy would have a drink on him as he was never without a bottle. Knowing Chancy's usual location, he quickly made his way there. At length, he located Chancy sitting next to a dumpster in an alley behind a convenience store. As Andrew approached, the frail wisp of a man, barely weighing a hundred pounds looked up at him.

"Go way!" Chancy said his voice sounding rasp.

"Chancy it's me Andrew!"

Chancy scooted back toward the rear of the dumpster enclosure as Andrew came closer, eyeing Andrew cautiously.

"Andrew!" Chancy suddenly exclaimed. "Wha're you doin' wit dat sailor outfit?"

"Never mind," Andrew intoned. "You got some drink?"

Chancy lifted up a brown paper sack containing a bottle of wine. He shook it to gauge the amount remaining in the bottle.

"Yas, ther's abit in'er. What cha got fer it? Some money?"

"Yes," Andrew replied, as he withdrew several dollar bills from his pocket, handing them the Chancy.

"Wat a minit," Chancy said before relinquishing the bottle. He took the cap off the bottle, placed it to his mouth and took a long drink. Seeming satisfied, he handed it to Andrew.

Andrew grabbed the bottle, looked around then quickly took a long swig.

It was the usual cheap low grade wine. As the alcohol entered his bloodstream, it began to warm him, and stopping the onslaught of the DT's. Having taken the drink, he quickly departed from Chancy and headed for an alley to get out of the publics view. Arriving at his destination, Andrew sat down and gulped the wine in a manner as though his life depended on it.

He finished the bottle quickly. It was not near the amount of alcohol he was use to consuming by this time of the day, although it gave him what his body was demanding.

Satisfied this would last him for the time being, Andrew got up and headed for the scrap yard. He wondered if Marty would be able to smell the booze on him.

Andrew arrived at the scrap yard. It was not open. He sat down by the front gate and waited for Marty.

CHAPTER THREE

ANDREW SAT ON a discarded pail, patiently waiting for Mr. Fieldman to arrive. The slight buzz created by the wine began wearing off. Chilled by the cold wind, he stood up and started pacing the sidewalk to generate some heat.

He was a block away from the scrap yard when a truck drove up to the gates. From the distance he recognized Mr. Fieldman as he got out of the truck cab.

Andrew quickly walked to the gates, reaching them just as Marty was unlocking a padlock. Marty glanced at Andrew when he had reached him.

"Can I help you?" Marty asked.

"It's me! Andrew, Mr. Fieldman."

"Andrew!" Marty exclaimed, "Sorry. I didn't recognize you without that scruffy beard. You look much better. Yes much better. Give me a hand latching these gates back."

The two latched the gates in position, got into the truck and drove to the weigh shack and stopped. After getting out of the truck cab, Marty walked around to the passenger side, opened the door and withdrew a money sack from the glove compartment.

He motioned for Andrew to follow him into the weigh shack. Unlocking and opening the door, they both stepped inside. Marty closed the door, locked it and then went to the cash register.

Andrew watched as Marty unzipped the money bag and removed all of its contents. Andrew's eyes widened as Marty sorted the bills, placing each one in their assigned compartments. Andrew was agog. He had never seen so much money in one place at one time. Marty noticed Andrew, sensing his amazement.

"Since I deal in cash, I have to have plenty on hand," Marty said casually."

Andrew continued watching Marty going about his task. When finished, he turned to Andrew.

"Well I must say again, you look much better without that scruffy beard and you smell a lot better. Where did you clean up?"

"At the YMCA. Slept there last night," Andrew replied.

"Good! Probably the best place for you since I'm sure you don't have a place of your own. Look, while I'm getting ready, make us some coffee. The pot's in the back room. I'll get the stove going."

Andrew walked to the back of the room, gathered the coffee pot and coffee ground basket, and set about making coffee. Mr. Feldman got the stove fired up, then continued getting ready for the days business.

Andrew returned to the stove and waited for further instructions from Marty. Suddenly there came a tapping noise on the service window.

Marty glanced out the window. "Uh Oh! Looks like trouble," Marty said as a pot marked faced man peered through the window into the room. The man was large in stature, easily able to tear either of the two apart. Andrew turned his attention toward Marty.

Marty unlocked the side door and stepped outside. He walked to the front of the weigh shack, stopping in front of the service window. Due to the sparse insulation in the weigh shack, Andrew could hear their conversation.

"What are you doing here?" Marty questioned.

"I've come back to work," the man said.

"Forget it! I gave you enough chances. You're always late and you miss too much work. I need someone who is reliable. Someone I can trust."

"But I was sick," the man said in defense.

"Sick? You weren't sick. You were full of booze. I've smelled alcohol on your breath many times even though I told you I didn't want alcohol in you while you were working here, I chose to ignore it, hoping you'd get my message about coming to work half plastered. You can just get out of here and don't come back. I hired someone to replace you."

The man stepped up to the window and peered inside the weigh shack. He glared at Andrew standing near the stove.

"Who do you have?" he asked, as he tried to get a better look inside the shack at his replacement.

"It's none of your business," Marty said.

"Honest Mr. Fieldman. I'll quit drinking. Just give me another chance," the man pleaded.

"Too late," Marty retorted. "Now you just get off my property."

Marty was about to turn and walk back into the weigh shack, when the man took a swing at him. Marty ducked and as rapidly as he could, entered the weigh shack, quickly locking the door. He withdrew a hand gun from a chest holster. The un-welcomed man tried to open the door but finding it locked gave up.

Marty yelled through the door. "You'd better get off my property or I'll call the cops. You know I carry a gun on me and not hesitate to use it."

The man banged and kicked at the door. "I'll get even with you, and that new man you got, I'll get even with him too."

As Marty removed his coat, he motioned for Andrew to keep silent. After a few minutes, he heard the crunching of gravel. Looking out the service window, he was relieved to see the man was departing the scrap yard.

"How do you like that?" Marty said angrily. "The damn alcoholic! I've given him a job, clothes and even a place to stay. Look how he repays me."

Marty limped over to the stove to warm up.

"I'll tell you right now, I'll not tolerate any booze, coming to work smelling of alcohol or not being able to work because of hangovers. You understand?"

"Yes sir," Andrew replied apprehensively. He was surprised Marty appeared to be venting his anger out on him.

The steam vapors from the coffee pot rose, permeating the room with the smell of fresh brewed coffee.

"You want some coffee?" Marty asked, as he picked up the coffee pot.

"Yes," Andrew said quietly.

Marty grunted in recognition, still angry over the intrusion by his former employee.

The two stood by the stove, enjoying the coffee and the warmth radiating from the pot belly stove. No words were exchanged between them. Marty eyed Andrew carefully as he sipped from his cup. Andrew avoided making eye contact with him.

The room began to warm from the heat of the stove, removing the chill that had filled the shack earlier. Marty was about to say something to Andrew, when he suddenly caught sight of someone outside the service window. He walked up to it and looked outside carefully, anticipating the huge man had returned.

He muttered something to himself. "Come up here Andrew," he called, while still peering out the window.

Andrew set the cup down and joined him.

"Look!" Marty said. "It's another one of those damned derelicts, just barely able to stand up."

Andrew cringed as he glanced out the window. It was Chancy toting a sack.

"Go out there and see what that bum wants."

Andrew put his cap on, unlocked the door, opened it and stepped outside. When he reached Chancy, he tried to keep his face hidden. He held out his hand as he approached Chancy. "Let me have your sack," he said when he reached Chancy."

Chancy handed Andrew the sack. Andrew quickly opened it, noting its contents then placed it on the scale and waited. After a few seconds a buzzer rang by the scale. Andrew did not know what it meant. He waited.

Marty opened the service window and yelled out. "Okay Andrew, dump those cans in the container. Be sure there are only aluminum cans in the sack."

"Zat you, Andrew?" Chancy asked, still slurring his speech after hearing Marty address him.

Andrew turned his back toward the weigh shack.

"Yes, but don't say anything to my boss," he said, while motioning his head in the direction of the weigh shack.

"Zo K, I won't," Came Chancy's' giddy reply.

"How long you been workin ere?"

"Just a couple days," Andrew answered, trying not to prolong the conversation.

"Makin lotsa cash?" Chancy asked.

"Enough," Andrew replied as he emptied the sack into the barrel.

He handed Chancy his empty bag and started walking toward the door. Chancy followed him like a puppy dog eager to learn more about his job.

"So dats how you got the loot to buy my stuff this morin."

"Yes!" Andrew replied, appearing annoyed. "You stop by the window and the man will give you your money."

"Yeah, sure," Chancy said, as Andrew quickly stepped back into the weight shack.

Chancy stood outside the window and waited patiently for his money. Marty motioned for Andrew to come up to the counter.

"I forgot to tell you about the buzzer," he commented. "It means the scale has finished weighing whatever was put on it. When you hear the buzzer, you can take the stuff off the scale. I had the automatic feature of weighing and figuring the payout amount fixed yesterday while you were unloading the truck."

Marty reset the counter on the readout panel mounted next to the service window. His position blocked Chancy's' view into the weigh shack. Andrew could see Chancy's' head bobbing up and down. From the corner of his eyes, Marty noticed his antics.

Marty opened the window. "What the hell is the matter with you?" Marty asked.

"Oh, nutin," Chancy replied, winking at Andrew after catching his glance

Marty turned and looked at Andrew. Turning back around, he opened the cash drawer and removed some bills and change.

"Here's your money," he said, handing it to Chancy.

Chancy carefully took the money and counted it. He put the bills and loose change into a small cotton sack he removed from his pocket. Closing the sack he tied it around a rope he used as a belt and stuck it inside his pants so as to be out of sight. He closed his coat about him, turned and began walking away from the weight shack. Marty shut the window and returned to the stove. Retrieving his cup, he poured himself more coffee.

Andrew watched through the window as Chancy slowly walked toward the gates. Halfway there, he turned around, catching sight of Andrew watching him. Chancy took both hands and patted his coat pockets. He then gave him thumbs up sign. Andrew knew that it meant Chancy was carrying several bottles of booze. Inwardly, Andrew was elated at this signal as Chancy was often his source of alcohol when he was unable to get his own.

As Chancy disappeared through the gate to be lost among the crowds, a large truck entered the junk yard. Andrew turned toward Marty. "There's a truck coming," he said.

"Good," Marty replied. "It's time to get to work."

Marty glanced out the window, surveying the approaching truck.

"That's one of Mr. Goodwin's trucks. It's usually loaded with different kinds of scrap metal. We'll have to separate and weigh each piece. As he spoke, the regular cashier opened the door and stepped inside.

"Good morning Marty," young attractive women in her thirties called out.

"Morning," Marty replied. "How's your mother doing?"

"She's much better now. I took her to the doctor yesterday and he gave her some medications."

"Good, good," Marty said. He motioned toward Andrew. "This is Andrew. I hired him yesterday to replace Quincy."

"Hey Andrew," the women greeted. "I'm Ellen."

Andrew recognized her from previous visits to the scrap yard.

"Hi," he replied.

Marty got his coat and put it on. "Follow me," he commanded as he passed Andrew.

He stepped outside and walked to the drivers' side of the truck, Andrew following closely behind him. The driver rolled down the window.

"Shamus!" Marty exclaimed, surprised at seeing him behind the wheel. "You are driving your own trucks now?"

"Just this once," Mr. Goodwin replied. "My driver had a sudden emergency and the others are busy. I need this truck for another job and can't wait for my driver to get back, so here I am."

"I see," Marty replied. "Okay, you know were to go."

Mr. Goodwin rolled up the window, put the truck in gear and drove further into the yard. He stopped in front of a large shed. Turning off the motor, he waited.

When Marty and Andrew arrived at the shed, Mary motioned for Andrew to jump onto the back of the truck.

"Pull that tarp back toward the front of the truck so Mr. Goodwin can dump his load," Marty instructed.

After Andrew pulled back the tarp and jumped off the truck, Mr. Goodwin engaged the hydraulic system raising the dump bed to unload the truck. Marty gathered some scrap lumber and tossed it into a nearby barrel charred from previous use. Picking up can of kerosene near a lean-to, he unscrewed the cap and poured some of it over the scrap lumber. Withdrawing a match, he lit it, stepped back and threw the match into the barrel. With a sudden swoosh the wood was completely engulfed in flames. The flames rose several feet into the air above the container. As the kerosene burned off, the flames died down, the fire now limited by the confines of the barrel.

"That'll provide some heat to keep the chill off you," he said. "Meanwhile, start sorting the metal into piles by type. I've got business matter to talk over with Mr. Goodwin."

Mr. Goodwin, a small pudgy man walked to the barrel. For a scrap dealer, he was impeccably dressed. His white hair and mustache were neatly trimmed. He extended his well manicured hands over the fire while rubbing them. Marty joined him. The two were out of ear shot of Andrew.

"New helper?" Mr. Goodwin, asked as the two stood by the barrel.

"Yes, he started yesterday."

"What kind of worker is he?"

"So far so good. Only time will tell if he'll be of any benefit to us."

"For your sake, I hope so. You know how hard it is to find good workers these days. I suppose he's another one of those homeless people?" Mr. Goodwin asked, raising his eyebrow.

"Yeah, Shamus, yeah!"

"How long is this one going to stay? You go through helpers like a douse of salts."

"I know, but I'm hoping he'll stay on."

"Hm!" Mr. Goodwin mused. "I don't know why you put up with these people. Why don't you just hire an illegal and be done with it. You know they're good workers and will do just about any job and for low wages."

"I prefer to help our own," Marty replied. "But if it comes to that I will, besides this one I want to keep."

"Oh?" Mr. Goodwin quizzed."

"He's kin," Marty said sternly.

Mr. Goodwin brushed at his mustache. "I hope you know what you're doing. I mean hiring kin, but it's your operation, not mine to question your decisions."

Noticing Andrew had finished sorting the scrap metal, Marty excused himself, walked up to a battered metal cabinet and withdrew a metal object. He returned to where Andrew standing.

"This is a magnet," he said, as he held it for him to see. "It's used to determine if metal is ferrous or nonferrous."

"I know what a magnet is, Mr. Fieldman," Andrew quickly replied.

"Good! Then you know how to use it?" he asked.

"Yes sir," he replied, taking the magnet from Marty.

Andrew picked up a piece of metal and put the magnet to it. It stuck. "This is ferrous metal, steel, iron?" he eagerly announced. He tossed it back onto the pile, and then selected another piece of metal. Once again he put the magnet to the metal but this time it didn't stick.

"This is nonferrous metal, like brass, copper, aluminum. Aluminum is silver in color and copper and brass have different shades depending on copper content," Andrew said, smiling as Mr. Fieldman looked on.

"Wonderful? Since you appear to know different types of metal, what I need you to do is weigh each piece making sure you press the correct metal type button."

Marty showed Andrew the scale, how to use it, and which buttons to press depending on what type metal he was weighing. When finished showing him, Andrew quickly set about weighing the metal. Marty watched him carefully, assuring himself Andrew knew what he was doing.

An hour passed and when the job was finished, Marty motioned Andrew to walk with him to the weigh shack. He continued instructing Andrew about the various tasks he wanted him to do. Mr. Goodwin slowly followed behind them in his truck. When the two reached the shack, Marty unlocked the door and the two stepped inside.

Mr. Goodwin stopped his truck in front, got out of the cab and walked to the service window. Marty looked over the figures on the digital readout and input some additional number, instructing Andrew all the while.

The scale made its computations, printed out a receipt which indicated the weights, metal types and amount to be paid. Ellen noted the cash amount to be paid. She unlocked the cash register, withdrew the money noted on the print out and handed it to Mr. Goodwin.

"Good load," Marty commented.

"Thanks! Will you need me to fill in for you anytime during the week?" Mr. Goodwin asked.

"Hm! I don't think so. I'll give you a call if I need you."

Mr. Goodwin got into his truck and headed toward the gates.

Marty watched, until the truck was absorbed by the busy traffic flowing past the scrap yard.

He turned to Andrew. "Sometimes Mr. Goodwin fills in for me if I'm going to be away or have other business to tend to in town. He's part owner of this business and fills in for me occasionally."

More trucks loaded with scrap metal followed. Andrew became engrossed in his chore of unloading, weighing and sorting as each truck entered the scrap yard.

He had just completed weighing a truck load of scrap, when a buzzer sounded near the scale he was using. It was a different sound, not familiar to him. Looking for the source of the buzzer, he was startled at hearing Marty voice, knowing he was in the weigh shack.

"Andrew!" he called. "Come up to the weigh shack."

Andrew scratched his head and walked to the weight shack. Arriving, he stepped inside.

"Sorry about the intercom," Marty said, "I forgot to tell you about it. Whenever I need you, I'll ring the buzzer and tell you what I want."

He had Ellen give him some cash, and then handed it to Andrew.

"Here, go to the deli and get us a sandwich, and one for Ellen. This time you won't have to worry about getting ripped off. I had a talk with the owner of the deli, a good friend of mine."

Andrew took the money and carefully put in his inside pocket, departed the weigh shack and headed out of the scrap yard.

As he walked, he felt proud, pleased with himself in showing Mr. Fieldman he could do the job. Silently he thanked him for the chance he was giving him.

Walking onward, he decided not to take the same route to the deli he had used the previous day. Remembering a shortcut, he decided to take it instead. The alternate route required traveling questionable alleys occupied by various derelicts. Andrew gave this little thought, as he often used alleys as a means of getting around the city.

Preoccupied with thoughts of the advances he appeared to be making, he was not paying attention to his surroundings. Traveling halfway through one of the alleys, he suddenly became aware of someone behind him.

Fearful of a confrontation, Andrew quickened his pace, but it was to no avail. Without warning there came a hard blow to the back of his head. Sparkles appeared in his eyes, as he heard someone yell. At the moment, everything went black. He fell to the ground, his body motionless.

Several minutes passed before he was able to regain any degree of consciousness. As he began to come to, his vision, now blurred from the blow to his head, revealed the outline of someone standing over him.

His head ached. He tried to get up when a voice faintly familiar to him instructed him to stay put. He waited until he regained full use of his senses. Looking up from the ground, to his surprise, he recognized Chancy stooped over his prostrated body.

"Chancy? Is that you? What happened?"

"Some big guy came up behind you and hit you on the back of the head. He hit you just as I was coming into the alley. It's a good thing I did or you'd be a goner."

Andrew sat up, trying to recollect what had happened. "I remember somebody yelling just before the lights went out. Was that you?"

"Yeah, that was me. Just as that guy hit you, I yelled. I suppose my yellin startled him because he ran away. He didn't have time to rob you."

Andrew reached his hand inside the pocket containing the money. It was still there. He felt relieved. Still groggy, he stood up with the help of Chancy. Wobbling a little, he managed to balance himself. He felt the back of his head.

"You gonna be alright Andrew?"

"Yes. I think so. There sure is a big bump on the back of my head. Is there any blood?"

Chancy inspected the back of Andrews head.

"No. Don't see no blood, but boy do you have a goose egg back there."

Andrew continued rubbing his head. The two started walking slowly out of the alley. By the time they reached the main street, Andrew felt recovered from the attack, as he was able to stand and walk without any trouble. Chancy appeared anxious to get on with his daily routine and drinking.

"If you're okay Andrew, I mean if you don't mind, I gotta run."

"You go if you have to, and listen, thanks for the help Chancy. You probably saved my life."

Chancy quickly darted back down the alley, the bottles inside his coat pocket clanking together as he departed.

Andrew turned and continued on his interrupted trip to the deli. His head still ached from the blow. Never had he felt such pain. It was worse than that of a hangover.

After reaching the deli, he made his transaction and headed back to the scrap yard with the sandwiches, along with the promised money he had been cheated out of the previous day. He was happy finding that the beer bellied counter man he met the day before was no longer at the deli.

Leaving the deli, he traveled the longer route, assuring himself he would be safe. Preoccupied with the attack, he was unconcerned about how he appeared to others. Without realizing it, for the first time he did not try to evade eye contact of others as he walked past them. He was too angry at being attacked.

He quickly walked into the scrap yard and to the weigh shack. Opening the door, he stepped inside. Marty was sitting on a chair next to the pot bellied stove reading a newspaper. He looked up at Andrew as he stepped inside.

"That was quick," Marty said, as Andrew closed the door.

Andrew did not acknowledge his comment. He handed Marty the sandwiches and change, then walked to the back of the shack. After hanging his coat on a nail, he returned and stood in front of the stove.

Marty watched him. He sensed something was wrong. Without saying a work, he handed him one of the sandwiches, then gave one to Ellen. Andrew took the sandwich but instead of eating it, he set it down on the shelf next to the coffee cups.

Marty returned to his newspaper, removed the wrapper from his sandwich and took a few bites, occasionally glancing at Andrew.

Andrew reached up and rubbed the back of his head, grimacing when he touched the bump.

Marty set his sandwich down. "What's wrong Andrew? Are you not feeling well?"

"I have a bad headache," he said.

Marty observed Andrew a while longer. Finished eating, he threw the wrapper into the trash can, walked over to the coffee pot and poured himself a cup of coffee.

Andrew felt his eyes watching his every move. He evaded eye contact with Marty.

"Okay Andrew. Let's hear it. What's wrong?"

Andrew was ashamed. He put his hands to his face and began to sob. He turned his back toward Marty, not wanting him to see his weakened state.

"Mr. Fieldman, I was attacked on my way to the deli," he finally volunteered. "Someone hit me on the back of the head while I was walking through an alley."

Marty almost dropped his coffee cup. He walked up to Andrew.

"Let me see," he said.

Andrew let Marty examine the back of his head.

"I don't see any blood, but there is a sizeable lump back there. I can imagine the pain you're experiencing."

He patted Andrew on the back.

"Everything will be fine. Things have a way of working themselves out. Just give it time. I've got something in the back that will help you with the pain. Eat your sandwich."

Marty walked to the back room.

Andrew began to feel better. He surmised, although Mr. Fieldman had a gruff demeanor, it appeared he was more concerned about his fellow man than he let on.

Andrew recalled the earlier events of the day. The help given for the loss of his shoes, the assistance of the attendant at the desk the night before and the help of the volunteers from the USO. Despite his inner belief, Andrew finally realized that some people do have true feelings for one another if you gave them a chance to express it.

Marty returned. He handed Andrew two capsules and a glass of water.

"Here, take these. They'll help relieve the pain."

Andrew looked at the pills questionably.

"They're pain pills. They'll make the pain go away."

Andrew put the pills in his mouth and took a drink of water.

"You'd better sit down," Marty said. "Those pills are powerful."

Andrew walked over to a chair near the stove and sat down.

"You just rest a bit. Besides, you won't be much use to me for the rest of the day after taking those pills. I'll get one of the other men to fill in for you."

Andrew looked at Marty. His expression was blank. He wondered what he meant by him not being much use to him. He wanted to go back to work, to show Marty he was capable of doing whatever he wanted. He was grateful Marty was giving him a chance, and a means to get out of the gutter.

"Mr. Fieldman, my work. I've got to show you I can do the work."

Marty smiled. "I know you're capable of doing the work. There's plenty of time. Besides, you've already shown me what you can do this morning. You just rest now, you've had a severe blow."

He watched Andrew carefully as he talked to him. As the pills began to take effect, Andrew became light headed, the pain slowly disappearing. Before he knew it, Andrew was in another world, unaware of what was going on around him.

Marty took hold of Andrews arm and instructed him to follow. He carefully led him to a separate small building a short distance from to the weigh shack.

Inside the building was a day bed. Marty took off Andrew's coat, and then helped him lay down. Seeing he was at rest, he closed the door. Andrew fell fast asleep.

CHAPTER FOUR

IT WAS THE most peaceful sleep he had ever experienced. It was the sleep of innocence. Several hours passed before he was to awaken.

He woke to a semi-darkened room. He sat up in the bed, not sure of where he was. Though dusk, his eyes slowly focused to reveal the inner confines of the room. When his eyes became accustomed to the dim interior, he was able to make out the layout of his surroundings.

In the far corner was a small stove. It had been filled with wood and lit. The fire provided took the chill out of the room. Opposite the stove was a small cubicle. Getting up, he walked over to it. Peering inside, he saw it was a small bathroom with a commode and sink. He noticed a stall, surrounded by a canvas curtain. He parted the curtain to reveal a shower.

He scratched his head, wondering where he was. As the light outside the cabin began to fade, he scanned the walls noticing a light switch and flipped it on. Instantly the little cabin was filled with a light from a single bulb hanging in the center of the room. He shaded his eyes from its harsh glare.

He looked around. Though rough in form, the cabin provided comfort. Andrew sat on the bed. How did he get here, he questioned. He could not remember any events since Marty had given him the pills.

Although groggy, he felt good, much better than he had in years. On a night stand next to the bed rested an old radio. He reached over and switched it on. After a few moments, music emanated from it.

Noticing a lamp on the headboard of the bed, he switched it on then turned off the harsh light hanging in the center of the room. The reading lamp provided much softer lighting.

"Much better," he said happily.

In a far corner, he noticed a refrigerator. There was a note tapped to the door. He got up and read the note. It was from Marty, instructing him to eat when he felt hungry. Opening the door, he peered inside. To his surprise, there were cold cuts, bread and condiments.

Andrew was delighted. He was hungry. Without hesitation, he fashioned himself a sandwich, returned to the bed and ate.

Lying back down after finishing his sandwich, he continued listening to the music. He had not given any thought to leaving the cabin.

Turning his head on the pillow, and glancing at the radio, he noticed a piece of paper sticking out from beneath it. Curious, he sat up, lifted the radio and took the piece of paper from under it. Unfolding the paper he began to read.

"Andrew. I put you in this cabin for the night because of the pills I gave you. It has all the comforts you might need. I will see you in the morning." The note was signed, Marty

Andrew's thoughts were in turmoil. Years of abuse made him a bitter man. He had long come to the conclusion that no one cared about him and that no one ever would.

The actions of Marty proved his thinking was wrong. He knew he had to do some soul searching and realized there were decent people in the world and Marty was one of them. He decided once again, he would do everything in his power to better himself, quit the booze and become part of the productive society. This he felt he owed to Marty.

Elated over the events of those who had helped him the past few days and for the decision he made, he wanted to tell the world. Jumping up, he ran over to his coat, took it off the hanger and donned it.

Rushing to the door, he tried to open it, but the door knob would not turn. Puzzled, he tried again, but it would not give in to his attempt to open it. It was locked from the outside.

Andrew took his coat off and returned it to the hanger. He stood pondering the situation. He wondered why the door was locked.

Returning to the bed, he laid down. He was distraught, confused. Why the prisoner, he asked himself. Still somewhat disoriented from the pills. He closed his eyes and continued listening to the radio. In a short time, he fell asleep, not to awaken until the next morning.

Andrew woke refreshed. His head was clear and without the usual day after grogginess experienced in the past. He could not recall when last he had felt so good.

After washing and shaving, he pondered his reflection in the mirror. He felt a sense of pride in himself and at the accomplishments he had made so far.

Finished in the small bathroom, he walked into the cabin and looked around, musing over its appearance. A single window let sunlight into the room.

The fire in the little stove had died out during the night, chilling the cabin. He put his coat on and headed for the door, stopping short of it when he passed the window. He peered outside. A short distance from the little cottage stood the weigh shack. He observed smoke coming out of the metal flue protruding through the roof. Marty's truck and Ellen's car was parked at the side. At the door, he stopped, recalling his attempt at opening it before falling asleep. Cringing, he put his hand on the knob to turn it. To his surprise, the knob relented. Andrew opened the door.

He quickly stepped outside, closed the door and swiftly walked to the weigh shack. Reaching it, he opened the door and stepped inside.

Marty glanced over at him as he entered.

"Did you have a good night's sleep?"

"Yes, Mr. Fieldman. Yes I did!"

"Good, but please start calling me Marty."

Andrew smiled and nodded, hung up his coat and got a cup of coffee.

"Just so you'll know, I had to lock the cabin door for your protection. Those pills I gave you yesterday, besides reliving pain, tend to make one disorientated. I didn't want you roaming around the scrap yard, much less the streets. You might have hurt yourself."

"That's okay, Mr . . . Marty," Andrew replied, relieved at his explanation for being locked in the cabin.

Andrew stood next to the stove, warming himself, as Marty went about his morning routine getting ready for the day's business. He was overjoyed and anxious to get back to work.

Finishing his coffee, Andrew rinsed the cup and put it back on the shelf.

"Is there anything I can do Marty?" he asked, eagerly.

Marty turned around and smiled. "Yes. Go down to the scrap pile you were at yesterday and get the fire barrel going. It won't be long until we start getting busy. Today is going to be the busiest day of the week. Wednesdays usually are."

Andrew put his coat on and left the shack. Reaching his destination, he gathered some wood, put it into the fire barrel and lit it in the same manner as Marty had done the day before.

Standing by the barrel, he scanned the surroundings of the scrap yard. Occasionally a worker in the distance caught his attention by the flash of light from a cutting torch the worker was using. The man was cutting away at larger pieces of scrap metal, making smaller pieces so they could be easily handled. Andrew watched and waited until he was needed. Abruptly the buzzer rang. Andrew turned around, facing the intercom. As expected, Marty's voice emanated from the speaker.

"Andrew, there's a truck on its way down to you. Unload it and separate the metals like you did yesterday. Be extra careful, the man is very picky and he will watch you like a hawk."

After several minutes waiting, the truck promised, slowly pulled up to where he was standing. The driver maneuvered his truck into position and turned of the engine. He got out of the cab and walked over to the barrel.

"Good morning," the driver, a large black man greeted.

"Good morning, sir," Andrew replied, surprised that he was actually being greeted by a stranger.

Andrew quickly jumped up on the truck and started throwing the various pieces of scrap metal onto the ground. As best he could, he separated the scraps by appearance. An hour passed before the truck was unloaded. Finished with the unloading, Andrew set about determining the types of metal, weighing each piece and inputting the proper codes into the key pad just as Marty had done. He was thoroughly enjoying his newfound job. He began whistling as he continued with the work. The driver watched his every move. Completing the sorting and weighting, Andrew pushed a button that would announce to Marty that all the items had been weighed then waited. As expected, the buzzer rang again.

"Tell Mr. Jarvas he can drive up to the weigh shack," Marty instructed.

Mr. Jarvas acknowledged the message and nodded in recognition.

"Have a good day, Mr. Jarvas," Andrew said.

"You too," replied Mr. Jarvas, as he walked toward his truck. Reaching the cab, he climbed into it and started the engine. He did not put the truck into gear right away. A few minutes passed, the truck still did not move. Curious, Andrew walked to the driver's side of the truck.

When Andrew reached the door of the cab, Mr. Jarvas rolled down the window.

"Here," he said, reaching out his hand. "You did a good job. Here's a little something."

"Thank you," Andrew replied, as he received what Mr. Jarvas handed him.

Mr. Jarvas smiled, rolled the window up and put the truck into gear and headed for the weigh shack.

Andrew watched as the truck disappeared from his view. What a nice person, he thought. Andrew opened his hand to see what the driver had given him. To his amazement, he was holding a five dollar bill.

He stared at the bill, feeling joyful. He could not recall the last time someone had given him money without him begging for it. Carefully, he put the bill in his pocket and waited for the next customer.

As the morning wore on, more trucks made their way into the scrap yard and down to where Andrew was working, as before, he unloaded, separated, and weighted the metal.

Midday came swiftly. Andrew stood by the barrel, having just finished his job with another truck. Several minutes passed. No more trucks appeared. He occupied himself by playing with the magnet, then testing various pieces of metal to see if he could recognize its composition without using the magnet. He felt proud of himself, becoming good at identifying various metals without having to use the magnet.

Once again the buzzer rang, disturbing his train of thought.

"Andrew," Marty called, "It's time to get something to eat. Come up here."

Returning the magnet back in the cabinet he walked and half ran to the weigh shack. Stepping inside, Marty turned around.

"You're doing a great job. All my customers seem pleased at how you're handling your work. Keep it up and won't be disappointed."

Andrew blushed at hearing the compliment.

Marty opened the cash drawer and handed him the usual amount of money.

"Time for you to go to the deli," he said.

Andrew took the money, opened the door and made his way to get lunch. As he traveled to the deli, he smiled and greeted strangers. He was delighted when the strangers greeted and smiled back at him.

Despite his elation over the events of the past day and a half, the lack of alcohol he was use to having begun to rear its ugly head.

Andrew had not given alcohol any though, but to his dismay, his body began to rebel. As he walked onward, the desire became stronger and stronger. Fight as he would, the battle got the better of him.

He walked up Forth Street, stopping in front of the liquor store. He paused, staring at the entrance.

Shaking in anticipation, he finally opened the door and stepped inside as he had done many times in the past. The clerk behind the counter looked up, pondering Andrew for a moment as though inspecting him.

"Can I help you with something?" the young man finally asked.

"Yes. Just a minute! I want to look over the displays."

The clerk continued pondering him, while Andrew looked at the large selections of liquor on display. At length, he selected a bottle of wine.

"That'll be three seventy-five," the clerk said.

Andrew handed the clerk the five dollar bill given to him earlier. The clerk rang up the sale, put the bottle in a brown paper sack and handed it to Andrew along with his change.

Andrew quickly took the bottle and placed it in his coat pocket. Turning, he rushed out of the liquor store with his prize.

Evading the main streets, Andrew stepped into an alley. In anticipation, he became jittery, barely able to keep his hands from shaking. He removed the bottle of wine from his pocket. Fumbling, he almost dropped it while taking it out of the bag. With difficulty, he managed to get the screw cap off.

Putting the bottle to his mouth, he took a quick swig. The liquor traveled down his throat to rest in his empty stomach. He took another swig, this time a much bigger one. As he was so accustomed to feeling, a warm sensation came over him as the alcohol did its job of rapidly entering his blood stream.

He sat down, using the side of the building as a back support and continued his drinking spree until the contents of the bottle had been consumed. He tossed the empty bottle aside.

Satisfying his body's needs, he got up and continued with his chore at the deli, then returned to the scrap yard. Reaching the weigh shack, he stepped inside. As usual, Marty was reading the paper. He did not say anything, knowing he had to keep his distance from Marty for fear of him smelling the alcohol on his breath.

Marty paid little attention to Andrew. He ate his sandwich while reading the newspaper. With his stomach now full of wine, Andrew was not hungry. He made little effort at eating.

Andrew watched Marty. When the time was right, while Marty was busy and sure his view was blocked from him, he threw the sandwich in the trash can, being sure it was out of view by burying it under the existing garbage.

The lunch break was cut short by the appearance of two trucks coming into the junkyard.

"Time to get to work," Marty announced, noticing the trucks.

Andrew got his coat, departed the weigh shack, and returned to the work area he was at earlier in the day.

Undaunted by the effects of the wine, he managed to perform his job as expected. Although he wanted to be friendly and talk with customers as they arrived, he felt it best not to say anything, assured they would smell alcohol on his breath and mention it to Marty.

The afternoon appeared to go quickly as Andrew kept himself busy, not allowing himself any lax time. When the trucks appeared less frequently, he knew it would soon be time to end the days work.

He had not added anymore wood to the fire, figuring he would not need the extra heat as the day ended. In anticipation, the buzzer rang. It was Marty.

"Time to call it a day, Andrew. You can come up to the weigh shack."

Andrew complied. As he entered the weigh shack, Marty was in the process of putting the last of the cash from the register back into the money bag. Zipping it closed, he paused.

"Now, look at me. I've closed the bag without giving you your money," Marty said.

Marty reopened the bag and withdrew a twenty dollar bill.

"Here you go, Andrew. Your day's wages minus a few bucks for those clothes I gave you the other day."

He zipped up the bag again, and then unzipped it once more.

"Oops! Didn't pay you for yesterday."

Reaching inside the bag, Marty took out an additional ten dollar bill.

"Okay, this should take care of the work you did yesterday, he said as he handed him the additional money."

Andrew eagerly took the ten dollar bill, not caring he was only receiving a partial day's wages for the previous day. Marty scanned the inside of the weigh shack to be sure everything was secure. Satisfied, he turned to Andrew. "Get in the truck. I'll take you back to the YMCA."

Andrew hesitated a second. He did not want to go to the YMCA right away. His intent was to get to the liquor store before it closed.

Marty noticed his hesitation. "Well, what are you waiting for? Get into the truck. I'll be out in a minute, as soon as I lock up."

Without saying anything, he reluctantly departed the weigh shack and got into Marty's truck.

After a short time Marty climbed into the cab. Putting the key in the ignition, he started the engine, letting it warm a little, then put it in gear and headed out of the scrap yard. When they passed beneath the gates, Andrew got out, closed and locked the gates.

The trip to the YMCA was short. On the way they passed a liquor store. Andrew craned his neck to see if the store was still open. To his delight, he was able to see lights on inside the store.

Marty stopped in front of the YMCA. Andrew opened the door and stepped out. He walked toward the entrance, listening as he did to see if Marty was going to continue onward. Andrew was delighted as Marty put the truck in gear and took off, soon lost in rush hour traffic.

Andrew paused at the entrance of the lobby. Assured Marty was out of sight, he quickly turned around and started walking as fast as he could toward the liquor store a few blocks away.

The streets were crowed with pedestrians. He had to move in and out of the crowded sidewalks in an attempt not to bump into anyone. The liquor store was only two blocks away, but it might as well have been a mile. The only real obstacle in his path was having to cross the street to the other side.

Coming to a corner, he waited patiently for the light to change. Never had he imagined had there been so many cars and people. Several times, when there was a lull in the cars, he was tempted to dash across but noticing a police cruiser parked on the opposite side of the street, he thought otherwise.

At last the light turned in his favor. He crossed the street and headed straight to the liquor store. He was about to open the door, when the clerk inside turned the sign around to indicate it was closed.

Andrew panicked. He banged on the door to get his attention. The clerk glanced at him.

"Sorry fella," he said through the door, "we're closed for the night. Come back tomorrow."

Andrew banged on the door again. "Look! I have money! I'll pay extra."

The clerk unlocked the door. "Okay, but make it quick."

Andrew quickly grabbed two bottles from the display without realizing what they were and handed them to the clerk.

"That'll be nine bucks plus the extra you promised," the clerk said.

Andrew handed him a twenty dollar bill and quickly departed the store without asking for any change.

He rushed out of the store and hurried to the same alley he had been to earlier in the day. Frantically, he took one of the bottles out of the bag, untwisted the cap and placed the bottle to his mouth, taking a long swig. To his surprise, in his rush he had purchased whiskey.

His craving satisfied, he continued to drink the whiskey until he emptied the pint. He retrieved the second bottle, opened it and continued his drinking spree, though at a much slower pace. When finished, he tossed the bottle aside, got up and slowly, with a slight stagger, made his way to the YMCA. Reaching it, he opened the door, stepped into the lobby and made his way to the registration desk.

The clerk at the desk, remembering Andrew from two nights prior, handed him the registration card as before. The whiskey on Andrews' breath made the man flinch.

"Just sign it like you did the other night," he instructed.

Andrew took the pen from the clerk and scribbled on the form. Fumbling, he reached into his pocket and took out a ten dollar bill and handed it to the clerk. The clerk took the money, made change and handed five dollars to Andrew. After receiving his change, he turned and walked to the elevators.

Having ridden the elevator to the fifth floor and entering the dormitory, he stumbled around and selected an empty bunk. He plopped down onto it and passed out.

He awoke when the glare of the dormitory lights suddenly came on. He sat up in the bunk. His head was pounding and his stomach was queasy.

Head aching, he walked to the community bathroom. Fumbling, he retrieved a dollar bill from his pants pocket. Having entered the bathroom, he walked up to the door where an attendant was stationed and handed him the dollar. In exchange, the attendant gave him a towel, washcloth and small bar of soap.

Andrew headed to the shower room and selected a stall. Just outside the stall he put his clothes and shoes on a bench. Stepping into the shower, he turned the water on but did not close the canvas curtain completely. He showered, keeping an eye on his clothes and shoes.

Once showered, he quickly dried off and put on his clothes. Having finished dressing and while putting on his shoes, he noticed they were soiled. Picking up the towel, he began wiping off his shoes. While doing so, a stranger walked up and stood in front of him. Andrew looked up. Before him stood a huge man, with a pot marked face, evident he at one time had a bad case of acne. There was a scar from beneath his left ear all the way down to his neck.

"I know you," the man said, as he stood staring at Andrew.

"Pardon me?" Andrew replied.

"Yes. You're the one. You're the one who got my job."

Andrew was not sure but from the stranger's voice, he felt the man was the one who had the argument with Marty a few days earlier.

"I'm sorry but I don't know what you mean," Andrew said.

"Oh yes you do! You're the one who got my job at the junkyard. You're the one Marty hired. I know, because I've been watching you, following you."

A wave of fear came over Andrew. He felt sure this was the person that had attacked him in the alley. He watched the stranger carefully.

"You losing your job were your own undoing," Andrew retorted, trying to sound calm as he finished wiping his shoes.

Andrew stood up. The man stood his ground, trying to prevent Andrew from passing.

"Excuse me," Andrew said, as he tried to walk past him.

The man grabbed Andrew by the arm, "Look you. I mean to get my job back anyway I can."

Andrew broke loose from the man's grip and started heading toward one to the sinks. The man was about to make an attempt to punch him, when an attendant, much larger than the man grabbed his arm.

"Hold on mister," the attendant said, "If you've got a beef, you can settle it outside. Not in here."

The man relented. He glared at the attendant a moment then looked toward Andrew, who was busy combing his hair in front of a sink. Andrew watched the man through the mirror. The man shrugged his shoulder.

"I'll settle this score with you later," he said, as he passed him while walking out of the bathroom.

Several of the men in the bathroom glanced at Andrew. Seeing them watching him, he decided to forgo shaving and made a rapid exit.

Quickly departing the bathroom, he walked through the dormitory and out into the lobby. Standing with a small cluster of men, he waited for the elevator. He looked around to see if the man who had accosted him was among the group. He did not see him. He felt relieved yet apprehensive, not knowing what the man had meant when he said he would get even with him.

Andrew stepped into the elevator along with the others when it arrived. As the elevator started its decent, he once again felt queasy in the stomach.

When the elevator reached the lobby, Andrew filed out with the others. He quickly made his exit from the YMCA and headed for the scrap yard. Andrew paid little attention to those he passed as he made his way along the street; his mind was on the stranger and his throbbing head.

As he passed over the tracks, Andrew saw Chancy sitting on the sidewalk, leaning against a lamp post for support. He was not anxious to see Chancy however; there was no way to avoid seeing him as he had to pass him to get to the yard.

As expected, Chancy caught sight of Andrew as he drew nearer. It was obvious Chancy was drunk, as his eyes were typically glassy. He held a bottle of wine up toward Andrew.

"Andrew," he called, as he was about to pass him. "Ere, hava drink."

A drink was the last thing on Andrews' mind. The thought of liquor upset his stomach even more so. He stopped for a second and looked down at Chancy.

"Not now Chancy," he said, "I've got to get to work."

Chancy glanced at him. He declined to make another offer or comment. He stared quizzically at Andrew for a few seconds, and then took another swig from his bottle.

Andrew looked down at Chancy. He pondered the state Chancy was in and realized what he himself had looked like when he was in the same condition. He shook his head. Never again, he silently said to himself.

Andrew left Chancy to his bottle and continued toward the scrap yard. As he approached the gates, he noticed that they were opened. A sigh of relief came over him, as he did not care to have to wait outside in the cold.

Marty turned and looked at Andrew as he opened the door and stepped into the weigh shack. Andrew did not say anything. He took off his coat and hung it on the nail.

"Coffee's ready," Mary commented, as he went about his usual chores of getting ready for the days business.

Andrew did not make a reply to Marty's comment. The thought of coffee too made him all the queasier. His stomach churning, Andrew quickly headed for the small restroom. To his surprise, he began to heave, his head pounding all the more. He knelt in front of the commode, emptying all the contents of his stomach. It had been years since he had experienced a bout of throwing up.

Andrew finished emptying his stomach, got up and rinsed his mouth out with cold water. Tears came to his eyes as the severe throbbing seemed never-ending. He felt as through his head would explode.

He stepped out of the restroom, evading Marty's glance, taking his usual station near the stove. Sitting down, Andrew put his elbows on his knees and held his head. The throbbing was unceasing.

Without saying a word, Marty walked over to a small cabinet, withdrew a bottle of pills, opened the bottle and shook out two pills.

Returning the bottle to the cabinet, he walked over to Andrew and handed him the pills.

"Here, take these. They'll help relieve your headache."

Evading Marty's eyes, he took the pills, went to the restroom, and swallowed them with a glass of water. He returned and sat back down on a bench by the stove.

Marty, leaving Andrew to his suffering, called on the intercom for one of the other men to fill in for him. Andrew sat in silence, fearing to even look at Marty.

The morning wore on. As it did, the pain in his head began to subside. Several hours passed before he began feeling better. Relenting to his stomach's complaint of being empty, he got up and poured himself a cup of coffee. He stood by the stove, sipping from the cup. Marty turned and watched as the noise of the coffee pot being disturbed reached his ears.

"Feeling better?"

Andrew nodded, too ashamed to look at him.

"You know, that damn booze will kill you one of these days."

Andrew knew all to well the danger of drinking. Several of the street people he knew in the past had succumbed to alcohol and now lay in some unknown grave. He turned toward Marty.

"I tried, Marty. Honestly I tried. It's so difficult."

"Look! Andrew," he said. "You're a good worker. The best I've seen in a long time from the likes of you. You can make something of yourself but you've got to try."

"I want to. I really want to give it up."

"That's a start," replied Marty. "If you want to give it a serious try, then I'll help you but be warned, I'll only give you one chance."

Andrew could see Marty was sincere in wanting to help him overcome his addiction. Andrew put it in his mind that he would do whatever it took, whatever Marty wanted in helping him give up the booze.

Seeing he was feeling better, Marty sent him after the usual lunch order. Returning and after eating, Marty instructed him to go down to his work area to take care of the afternoon's business.

The afternoon went by quickly, as Andrew kept himself busy at his job. At days end, he stepped into the weigh shack. Marty noticed Andrew had a worried look on his face.

"What's the concern?" Marty asked, as Andrew took off his coat.

Andrew held his thoughts a moment before answering, trying to rationalize the events of the morning.

"I was approached by a stranger this morning at the YMCA. I think it was that guy who worked here before I did. The man said I took his job and he was going to get even with me."

"Quincy Roberts," Marty said shaking his head. "That's the man you replaced. I knew he was a hothead but never expected him to go this far. Tell you what, Andrew; I think it best if you lay low for a couple of days. You know, keep out of circulation. The best way I know of is if you stay here, inside the scrap yard."

Andrew was not quite sure if he was willing to do as Marty had suggested. The thought of being locked up, plagued his mind. To be what he imagined a prisoner inside the scrap yard did not set well with him. Andrew was his own prisoner, a prisoner to his habit, a prisoner to alcohol.

"Mr. Fieldman," he finally said, "I can take care of myself. I've been doing just that for the past twenty-five years. I'll be fine."

Relenting, Marty replied. "Okay, if that's your wish, I'll honor it but please be mindful of the alcohol. Keep off it. It'll only doom you."

Andrew looked down at the floor like a kid just caught with his hand in the cookie jar.

"Mr. Fieldman, I'm going to keep off the sauce. I promise. I just need some time to think, to clear my mind."

Marty went to the cash drawer, withdrew Andrew's wages for the day, and handed him his money.

"Where are you going to stay tonight?"

"There's a flea bag of a motel down the road a bit. I'll stay there instead of the YMCA. I'll be less likely to run into that Quincy fella, since he probably thinks I stay there all the time."

Andrew put on his coat and stepped outside the weigh shack. Marty watched as Andrew left the scrap yard. He shook his head, appearing disappointed Andrew did not take him up on his offer.

CHAPTER FIVE

ANDREW FELT DISAPPOINTED in himself for letting Marty down. He swore to himself he would do his best to keep off the booze, despite his inner desire to get something to drink. He refused to admit his addiction to alcohol was more than he could handle, and it would require the help of others.

He walked slowly along the sidewalk paralleling the scrap yard, stopping in front of a fast food restaurant. He contemplated whether to eat or give into his body's desire by turning around and heading to the liquor store. Now fully sober, his body pained him, begging for the alcohol fix. He closed his eyes tightly.

"No!" he said to himself. "I've got to do it."

He opened the door to the restaurant and stepped inside. He scanned the menu board hanging above the service counter.

"May I help you?" a young girl asked, while he studied the menu.

"Yes. I'll have a hamburger and a chocolate milkshake."

The young girl took his money and rang up the sale.

"If you'll sit down, I'll bring your order out to you," she said, as she handed him his change.

Andrew turned and walked to an empty table near one of the windows facing the street. Sitting down, he surveyed his surroundings. The only patrons beside himself were a young couple in a far booth.

Although early evening, it was already dark outside. Andrew looked at his reflection in the window. His unshaven face looked back at him. He gave thought to his appearance and made a mental note that he must shave. Recent experience made him realize ones appearance determines how you might expect to be treated by others. His thoughts were disrupted when the girl stepped up to the table.

"Here you go, sir," she said, as she set down a small tray with his order on it in front of him.

"Thank you," he said in a subdued voice.

The girl left him to his meal. He picked up the hamburger, removed the wrapper and began to eat.

Andrew continued looking out the window as he ate, watching the traffic and passersby. He did not give these any thought until he saw Chancy.

Chancy was staggering as he made his way along the street. Andrew knew Chancy was always good for a drink. He began shaking as the urge to get a drink became stronger, building up inside him as though he would explode if he did not give into his body's demand. He took a sip of his milk shake, his eyes fixed on Chancy.

Giving into the urge, Andrew was about to get up from the bench, when Chancy staggered out onto the street in the path of an oncoming car.

"Chancy!" Andrew yelled, as he stood up.

The oncoming car made a sudden stop, as the driver slammed on the brakes while laying on the horn. The young couple glanced at Andrew, and then turned their attention to the commotion unfolding outside as one car rear ended another.

It all had taken place in a matter of a few seconds. Andrew closed his eyes, knowing Chancy would be dead. He opened his eyes. He was afraid to move, to go look at the mangled body he imagined would be laying on the ground. He continued to watch as the lead driver got out of his car, running to the front of it.

The driver stood looking down at Chancy. He began yelling angrily. Stooping down, he picked up Chancy. Chancy staggered, barely able to keep his balance. Andrew was relieved seeing no harm came to him.

Andrew thought about going to his aid but held fast when he saw several police cars driving up and stopping where the lead car had made a sudden halt. Police officers hurriedly got out of their cruisers to survey the accident.

Two officers stood talking with the driver of the lead car as he described what had happened. He would occasionally point at Chancy while he spoke. After a few minutes of listening, one of the officers took Chancy by the arm and made him get into one of the police cars.

Andrews' heart sank, not only because Chancy would probably spend the night in the slammer, but due to his chance of getting drink vanishing.

He sat back down and continued to stare out the window, while unconsciously playing with the wax covered cup holding his milkshake. Taking a few sips, he watched as the police cruiser Chancy had gotten into drove off.

Just as well, Andrew thought. I didn't need the drink anyway.

Andrew could not finish his meal. He got up and gathered the remains of his supper. Walking up to a trash container, he put the remains of his half eaten hamburger and the remains of the shake into it.

Buttoning his coat, he opened the door and stepped out into the cold night air. The milkshake chilled his insides, making him feel all the more cold. He continued walking down the street, past the cars involved in the accident. He snickered to himself, thinking it amusing how one such as Chancy could be the cause of so much confusion.

Ahead of him, he could see the flickering sigh of a long neglected motel. At one time the motel was the pride of the road, frequented by the affluent of society. The new interstate, rerouting the bulk of traffic around the city and lack of business caused the motel to be sold and resold.

The present owner, someone more concerned about cash flow than the condition of the motel, used it as a tax write off. The motel had decayed to a point of being known as a place good for a one night stand or for the occasional use of vagrants who might have a little money to spend.

Andrew slowly progressed toward the motel. A block away, Andrew was about to pass a convenient store, when he happened to glance inside. Various neon signs advertised several brands of beer. He stopped and studied the signs.

Andrew had never liked beer. To him it was too bitter. He could not rationalize how anyone was able to acquire a taste for it. He smacked his mouth. Well, it's better than nothing, he thought and it won't harm me. It's only beer.

He walked up to the store, opened the door and stepped inside. Pausing near the front, he looked around. Toward the back he noticed the refrigerated cases displaying the various chilled beers. Walking up the coolers, he studied the multitude of brands. He didn't know one from the other. Scanning the prices, he selected a six pack of the cheapest he could find, walked to the cashier, paid the attendant, and then stepped outside.

Clutching the six pack under his arm and walking as quickly as he could, he finally reached the motel office. Opening the door, he stepped inside. A bell above the door jingled at the opening and closing of the door. There was no one inside the office. He stood and waited.

Several minutes passed before a short, fat, beer bellied man stepped up to the counter from behind a curtain separating the small office and a back room. He looked at Andrew.

"Yeah? What do you want? A room?" he asked, seeming bothered by having to service Andrew.

"Yes."

"For the night?"

"Of course," Andrew replied, somewhat bothered by his attitude.

The man wiped his hands on his dirty T-shirt while studying Andrew carefully. He stared at the brown sack under his arm. He picked up a registration card and was about to hand it to him but then put the card back down on the counter.

"Look," he said, "if you want a room with clean sheets, that'll be twenty bucks, and you'll have to fill out this registration, or I can let you have a room that's been used for a couple hours for five without registering."

"I'll take the five dollar room," Andrew said without hesitation.

Andrew took the remaining bills from his picket and counted out five dollars. The man took the bills and stuffed them in his pocket. He turned around, took one of the many keys from a peg board and handed it to Andrew.

"Room seventeen, in the back," he said, motioning in the general direction of the room.

Andrew took the key and stepped outside. He made his way to the back row of rooms, stopping when he came to the door marked seventeen.

Fumbling, he put the key in the lock and turned it. He hurriedly opened the door and went inside the room closing the door behind him. He reached up and felt for the light switch. Locating the switch, he flipped it on. A single lamp resting on a stand next to the bed lit the interior of the room.

Andrew tossed the sack on the unmade bed. He took off his coat and laid it over the back of the chair next to the window. The raged curtain covering the window was partially opened. He made an attempt to close the curtain completely but was unsuccessful. He sat on the bed and picked up the bag, opened it and took out the six pack of beer. Taking one of the cans off the plastic ring holding the cans together, he opened the tab and took a quick drink. He almost gagged as the beer traveled down his throat.

Over the initial shock of the first swallow, he continued drinking, not putting the can down until it was emptied. Having finished the contents of the can and seeing a small trash container in the corner of the room, he threw the empty toward it. The can missed the container and landed among sever other beer cans on the floor. Picking up the partial six pack, he pulled another off the ring and opened it.

He eyed the room. The walls were badly in need of repair. Several holes in the plaster were scattered at various places throughout the room. The wall paper was stained and pealing away near the door and window, damaged by water leaks.

Andrew took the two pillows and placed them at the head of the bed, fashioning a makeshift back rest. Climbing onto the bed he leaned against the pillows. Glazing up at the ceiling, the water stains caught his eyes. He stared at the ceiling, his mind blank, tracing the many cracks in the plaster.

Although not as strong as wine, the beer, having drunk his third, began to give him the buzz he was accustomed to and satisfied his body's demand for alcohol. Again he tossed the empty can in the general direction of the trash container, unconcerned as to where it landed. Becoming a little drowsy, instead of getting another can of beer; he closed his eyes and fell asleep.

A half hour passed when he was awakened by the slamming of a car door just outside his room. Andrew got up and looked out the window through the parted curtain. A man and women, both appearing drunk, got out of the car and headed to the room next to his. They laughed and carried on, making a din sure to keep their neighbors awake. Their voices became muffled as they entered the room next to his.

Andrew turned from the window and walked into the small bath room. Flipping on the light switch, he caught sight of cock roaches frantically scurrying around, trying to find a place to hide as though fearful the sudden light meant certain death. The room had a musty smell. He parted the shower curtain and glanced into the combination shower tub. As expected, the mold around the edges of the tile was visible.

Andrew sat on the commode. A roach ran between his legs. He made an attempt to smash it with his shoe but missed. The roach ran into a crevice in the wall, out of harms way. Finished, he got up. He reached for the handle and pushed it. Nothing happened. He tried again and again without any success. Instinctively, he took the lid off the back of the commode, reached his hand into the tank, and pulled at the chain. The commode flushed. He put the lid back on the tank, turned around and walked to the sink.

Once pure white porcelain, the sink had rust stains from the constant drip of water from the leaky faucet. He turned on the water, briefly put his hands under it, turned the faucet off and halfway dried his hands on the towels hanging next to the sink.

He walked back into the bedroom. As he passed the TV on a small stand near the foot of the bed, he turned it on. Standing, he waited until the picture unfolded on the screen. Flipping through the channels, he stopped at one that seemed interesting.

Returning to the bed, he turned off the lamp on the night stand. Reaching over to the night stand, he got another can of beer, pulled at the tab and opened it.

The light from the TV cast an eerie shadow throughout the room. Andrew watched as the actors went through their mundane routine of trying to please an unseen audience. Andrew glanced at the window once again. The yellow light from the bulb just outside the door penetrated into the room, shining on the head of the bed where he lay. He got up and again tried to close the curtain. The curtain would not close any further.

He lay back down on the bed and continued to watch the TV as he sipped another beer. Occasionally his peripheral vision caught someone walking past the window as the yellow light penetrating into the room would be broken. Each time this occurred, he would glance toward the window but was never able to see anyone. Feeling the interruptions were the results of the motel residents passing by his room, he put the incidents out of his mind.

Andrew continued drinking, until he came to the last can of beer. Aware this was his last, he drank slowly in an attempt to savor the remains of the alcohol. All too quickly he emptied the last can. Carelessly, he tossed the empty on the floor.

He had achieved what he had set out to, to give his body the alcohol it needed. Now feeling the full effects of the beer, he fell fast asleep.

Andrew was suddenly awakened by the feel of something beneath his chin. An intruder had entered his room and was straddled over him.

He looked up but could not recognize the intruder as the TV's harsh light only lit the back of the figure, making it difficult to see his face. Andrew felt the point of a knife under his chin.

Although groggy, he realized he was in danger.

"Look," Andrew managed to say, "all the money I've got is in my coat pocket. You can have it all."

The intruder did not make any comment to his plea, pushing the knife a little harder into Andrews chin. Andrew flinched, drawing back into the pillows in an attempt to keep the knife from penetrating his skin.

"What do you want?" he called out.

"You. I want you," the man said in a calculated voice.

"Why?"

"Why?" mocked the intruder. "Because you took my job, that's why."

Andrew searched his memory. Fearful, he realized it was the man who had approached him earlier in the day at the YMCA.

"You took my job," the man continued. "I told you I'd get even, and here I am to give you your just due."

Andrew tried to reposition himself. The intruder followed suit and kept the knife under his chin. Without the man noticing, Andrew managed to get his hand under one of the pillows he was laying on. With a sudden jerk, he pushed the pillow into the intruder face.

The man fought at the oncoming pillow. Andrew began to get up, when suddenly the knife was thrust into his side. Andrew cried out, falling backward onto the bed.

The intruder was about to thrust the knife again, when the occupants of the next room heard the commotion.

"What was that?" A voice called out.

The man quickly ran out of the room, leaving Andrew bleeding on the bed.

Andrew was in agonizing pain. He clutched his side in an attempt to keep the blood from flowing out of his body. He slipped into unconsciousness.

Andrew slowly opened his eyes. The bright light shining down from above the operating table into his eyes blinded him from seeing what was going on. Someone with a green mask covering their face looked down at him.

"He's coming to," an unfamiliar female voice said.

Another masked person walked over to the table and looked down at Andrew.

"You're going to be fine," a man assured.

Andrew was in the county hospital emergency room. The on-duty staff doctor went about his duty of patching Andrew up the best he was able. He had just finished suturing Andrews wound. He glanced down at him.

"We'll give you something for the pain," he said, then turned away from the operating table to tend to other patients.

A nurse with a syringe walked up to Andrew, rolled him on his side and gave him an injection. Within a few moments, Andrews' pain eased. He felt as though he was floating on a cloud.

Hazy as he was, he could feel his body being placed on a gurney positioned next to the operating table.

Secured to the gurney, an orderly rolled it down the corridor and into another room, stopping the gurney next to an empty bed. The orderly, along with a nurse, maneuvered Andrew's body until it was situated on the bed. Andrew fell into a comfortable sleep.

Several hours passed before he woke up. When he did, there was someone looking down at him.

"Hi!" Someone said as Andrew opened his eyes. "How do you feel?"

"Everything's fuzzy," he said, his speech slurred from the medication. He tried to see who was talking to him.

"That'll pass," the voice said, as someone squeezed his hand. "You just rest now. You've lost a lot of blood."

Andrew did not say anything further. He tried to recall what had happened and how he came to be in the hospital. He turned his head on the pillow, noticing several other beds besides his in the room. As his mind began to clear, he realized he was in a hospital ward.

Throughout the remainder of the night, he drifted in and out of sleep, although the bouts were restful.

Occasionally a nurse would come in, check on his condition. She would check the IV bottle and the needle in his arm then leave him to his rest.

Morning in the hospital came early for Andrew. When the lights in the ward were switched on, those not heavily sedated awoke to a rash of various hospital personnel entering the ward. Orderlies provided the necessary bedpans for each of the patients. Andrew hesitated when an orderly came up to him, offering a bedpan. He felt uncomfortable having to use one, but the need to make use of it was stronger than his embarrassment when the orderly sat him up in the bed and placed the bedpan under him.

Having finished, the young man took the bedpan away. Another orderly, in a professional manner, carefully changed Andrews' sheets with a minimal amount of disturbance. Andrew marveled at the routine and the attention being paid to him.

Pulling himself up to get into a better position, he felt a slight tinge of pain in his side. He looked down and saw the bandage around his waist. In the center there was a splotch of blood which had managed to penetrate the several layers of gauze.

Andrew looked at the bandage, puzzled at its presence. He still could not remember what had happened or how he came to be in the hospital. He lay back down. The effects of the medication began to wear off as the intensity of the pain in his side started to increase. He could now feel the IV needle that was stuck in his arm.

Half an hour passed when a group of men and women in white hospital smocks with stethoscopes around their necks walked up to the foot of the bed. Although difficult, he managed to look toward the foot of the bed to see what was going on.

One of the doctors picked up a chart attached to the railing at the foot of the bed and began reading what had been written on it.

"Here we have a stab victim, a John Doe," the doctor said, getting the attention of the others. "The patient was brought into the emergency room late last evening with a single laceration in his side. Even though the wound was deep and much blood was lost, the puncture did not hit any vital organs. This one was lucky."

The doctor put the chart down and walked to the bedside, looking down at Andrew.

"How do you feel?" he asked, as the others gathered around each side of the bed to observe.

"Except for the pain, I feel okay."

"We'll take care of the pain in a little while. Right now we need to get a look at that wound of yours. Can you manage to sit up?"

Andrew sat up, though he grimaced, because the pain was becoming unbearable. The doctor motioned for a nurse standing near a cart to come to the bed. The nurse pushed the cart up to the bed. She picked up a pair of scissors and cut the bandage wrapped around Andrews' waist. She carefully removed the bandage, discarding it in a plastic bag, allowing the wound to be exposed.

The doctor continued instructing the others, pointing out the size of the puncture and describing the wound in medical terms foreign to Andrew. He blushed as each intern in turn viewed the wound, asking questions and receiving replies from the doctor.

All the attention Andrew was getting was over in five minutes. The doctor told the nurse to put new bandages over the wound and watched as she performed her task. The nurse, having finished, departed the scene. Moving to the foot of the bed, the doctor picked up the chart and made some notations on it. Before he left Andrews' bed, he made one other statement that caused Andrews face to turn red.

"From the information gathered so far," the doctor said in a matter of fact manner, "this patient is a typical alcoholic. His blood alcohol was quite high when admitted into the hospital. His case is quite common here. One other point, you'll notice on his chart, he has a high white blood cell count. This is due to an unknown condition within the body. We'll make tests to determine the cause."

The doctor replaced the chart at the foot of the bed. The group departed, moving on to the next patient in the ward. Andrew felt hurt by what the doctor had told the others. He did not like being reminded he was an alcoholic and worse yet, for others to be told he was one.

Andrew laid back down in the bed. The pain became intense as he moved to get into a comfortable position. A short time passed when a nurse came to his bed side, carrying a tray with a syringe on it.

"Are you still in pain?" she asked.

Andrew nodded. The nurse picked up the syringe, held it upside down, and pushed on the plunger to remove the excess air. She walked over to the IV bottle and put the syringe into a little bulb attached to the IV and pushed on the plunger. The fluid from the syringe entered the bottle. She put the empty syringe down, then turned and opened a valve that let the fluid flow into the IV tube. Within seconds, the pain disappeared. A little while later Andrew became drowsy. He closed his eyes and fell into a deep sleep.

He had no idea how long he slept. He was suddenly awakened by a clanking noise. Opening his eyes, he looked up to see a nurse standing over his bed looking down at him.

"Good morning," she greeted with a bright smile. "Are you hungry?"

Andrew wanted to sleep, turning over in an attempt to evade her.

"Oh no you don't," she said, turning him over on his back. "You've got have same nourishment. You'll have to sit up so I can give you your tray."

He reluctantly obeyed the nurse, scooting himself up in the bed to a sitting position. She took his pillow and repositioned it to provide a better back rest. Then she put the tray on a stand and swung it over the bed so he could eat. Walking to the foot of the bed, she glanced at his chart.

"Is there someone we can contact who might be concerned you're here?" she asked.

Andrew gave her the information about Marty. She made a notation and continued reading the chart.

"Well, I'm sorry, I have to take you off the pain medication for a short period so the lab can take some test later," she said. "It has to do with your white blood cell count."

Andrew, still groggy, half heard what she said. He looked down at the tray with covered plates. Not accustomed to this type of treatment and never experiencing a meal in bed, he did not know what to do.

The nurse reached over and took off the cover used to keep the food warm. A breakfast Andrew had not seen in a long time was revealed. Scrambled eggs, bacon, toast, jam, orange juice and coffee lay before him.

"You go ahead and eat. I'll come back when you're through."

Andrew picked up the fork and began to eat.

Sated, Andrew leaned back against the pillow and looked at his surroundings. The ward had beds on each side of the room situated to provide a walkway down the middle. Every bed was occupied. One at the far end had the curtain pulled around the bed to keep others from seeing. He glanced at the IV bottle, watching the slow drip of liquid from the plastic sack travel down the tube into his arm. He wondered what was in the bottle.

A half an hour passed, when the nurse returned.

"Well, I guess we were hungry. You ate everything. That's a good boy," she said.

Andrew blushed. He felt like a child being rewarded for doing good.

The nurse winked at Andrew as she took the tray from off the stand. She set the tray on the chair next to the bed, went to the IV bottle and turned off the valve that permitted the pain medication to enter into the IV tube.

"I have to turn this off for the time being so we can get a blood test, and now it's time for your bath," she said.

His eyes widened. He quickly pulled the covers over his head.

"Bath?" he questioned.

"Yes. It's time for your bath. My, aren't we the bashful one," she said, as she pulled the covers down. "The orderly will be here shortly to tend to you. We can't have you smelling up the place." Andrew relaxed when she walked away with the tray.

"A bath?" he whispered. "She's not going to give me a bath."

Several minutes passed. A male orderly appeared at his bed, carrying a tray with a wash basin, soap, towels, and several other articles on it. He set the tray on the same stand used to hold the breakfast tray. The orderly reached up and pulled the curtain around the bed to provide some privacy. The curtain closed, he began to give Andrew a sponge bath. He felt embarrassed. The only person he could recall giving him a bath was his mother.

The orderly did not say a word. We went about his task in a professional manner. Andrews face reddened when the order was about to wash his private parts.

"Would you rather wash this area yourself?" he asked.

Andrew nodded. The orderly rinsed out the wash cloth, put some soap on it and handed to Andrew.

"Don't get your bandages wet," he said, as he stepped outside the curtain allowing Andrew to wash himself.

After several minutes passing, the orderly called through the curtain, "Are you through?"

"Yes," Andrew replied.

The orderly stepped inside the curtain and finished the bath. Andrew sat up against the pillow. Taking an aerosol can, the orderly put some lather on his hand, then applied it to his unshaven whiskers. Carefully he shaved Andrews face clean.

Having finished, the orderly opened the curtain, picked up the tray and walked away. He disappeared behind the double swinging doors leading into the ward.

A lab technician arrived and quickly took the blood samples ordered by the doctor.

Andrew did not quite know what to make of the situation. He still could not figure out how he came to be in the hospital. He searched his memory, trying to make sense out of what was happening. Nothing came to mind.

Several hours passed. He started to become restless, not being accustomed to being penned up. Several times he tried to get up from the bed, but the pain in his side became a constraint.

He attempted to get some sleep, but it was to no avail due to the intensity of the pain. He wondered when someone would come by and ask him about how he felt. No one came. He felt alone. For the first time in his life, he longed for some company.

Suddenly someone appeared at the foot of the bed.

"Hello, Andrew. How are you feeling?"

Andrew looked down toward the bottom of the bed. To his surprise, it was Marty.

"Mr. Fieldman," Andrew said, in a weak voice.

Marty walked to the head of the bed and sat on a chair next to it. He was wearing bib overalls and an army field jacket.

"Shh!" Marty motioned with his finger to his lips. "You mustn't exert yourself too much. You've had a bad blow."

Andrew was excited and yet depressed at the same time. He was happy Marty had shown up. Feeling ashamed, he turned his head away from him.

Marty reached up and took his hand and held it for a few moments. Andrew turned and looked at him.

"What happened?" Marty asked.

"I don't know, Mr. Fieldman. Honest I don't know. The last thing I was aware of was going to sleep in the motel room then waking up here."

"Somebody stabbed you, Andrew. Don't you have any idea of who or why?"

Andrew tried hard to search his memory. He could not remember.

"Okay," Marty said, "What was done, was done. I have an idea who might have stabbed you, but proving so, that's another thing. Nothing can undo the act. The important thing is that you get better."

Andrew smiled. The two looked at one another, not saying a word. Marty appeared to be in deep thought.

"Andrew," Marty said after a few moments. "Each of us is forced into this life. None of us asked to be put on this earth, to play the game we must go through, but it's up to each of us to make the best of our stay while we journey through our short stay here. Few of us have an easy life. Occasionally someone comes along and provides a lift that will make the path much easier for us to travel. In your case, I'd like to be the one to ease your burden."

"Why, Mr. Fieldman?" Andrew questioned, "Why? I'm nothing. A nobody! All I ever wanted to do is get a bottle."

"I have my reasons. It's something I must do for your sake. Besides, there is something you need to know and time you knew."

"I knew? I knew what?" Andrew questioned.

"In time, in time Andrew, but first let's get over this mishap. For right now, we need to get you out of this ward. I've arranged to have you put in a semiprivate room. The doctor tells me you need to have some test performed."

He patted Andrew on the arm. "I'll be back. You just rest and get better. We'll beat this thing."

As far as Andrew was concerned, he was getting the best care he had ever experienced. He did not know what Marty meant.

Marty got up and walked out of the ward. Andrew was puzzled. He still found it difficult convincing himself that anyone truly cared about him.

He attempted to rest the best he could, but the pain became unbearable. Attempting to sleep, he tossed and turned but could not find a comfortable position.

A nurse came to the bed. “Mr. Simpson, are you still in pain?” she asked.

Andrew turned toward her. He was barely able to reply.

“Yes,” he managed to say in a feeble voice.

“I’ll take care of that right away since the lab technician got your blood sample. We’ll put you back on the pain medication, but it will only be for a short time.”

The nurse walked over to the IV bottle and opened the valve that had been closed earlier. Within seconds he felt better. The pain slowly subsided.

He began to feel drowsy again. He looked up the nurse, trying to express his gratitude. She looked down at him and smiled.

You rest, Mr. Simpson,” she said. “If you need anything, just ring the buzzer pinned to your pillow when you get to your room.”

Several minutes later, he was fast asleep.

CHAPTER SIX

ANDREW SLEPT SEVERAL hours undisturbed. He awoke refreshed, yet still groggy from the medication seeping into his body from the IV bottle. As he lay on his back, he opened his eyes, turning his head to one side. A puzzled expression came to his face.

Instead of seeing the other beds next to his, he was glancing at a window. Startled, he rolled over on his side. To his surprise, there was a single bed was next to his. He was in a semiprivate room.

Having a need to relieve himself and while attempting to get up, one of the many leads attached to his chest became dislodged from a suction cup. He looked at the wires, wondering why they were there. Suddenly the door to the room burst open. In ran two nurses.

"Mr. Simpson, are you alight?" one of the nurses asked, noticing he was trying to get out of bed.

"Yes, I guess. I just wanted to get up and pee."

"You mustn't move. We'll get something for you to relieve yourself."

The nurse opened a little door in the night stand next to the bed and withdrew a portable, stainless steel urinal. She turned toward him.

"Here you go," she said. "You can use this."

The nurse moved to place the urinal where it needed to be.

Realizing what was about to happen, Andrew made an attempt to grab the urinal. Missing, he fell back down and looked up at the nurse, his face flushed.

"I can do it myself."

She smiled. "We'll wait outside until you're through. She opened the door, motioning for the other nurse to follow.

Andrew relieved himself. He set the partially filled container on the stand next to the bed and waited.

Several minutes passed when the door opened again. In stepped one of the nurses who had been in the room earlier. She walked up to him, picked up the lead that had fallen off the suction cup attached to his chest and replaced it.

"There," she said. "Now we'll know if you're alright."

Andrew looked at his chest, contemplating the leads. "What are these for?"

"They're so we can monitor your heart. The monitor is at the nurses' station."

He laid back on the bed and watched the nurse as she went about checking the IV bottle, the needle in his arm and bandages.

"How did I get in this room" he asked. "I was in a large room with other beds before I fell asleep."

"Mr. Fieldman requested that you be placed in a semiprivate room. He said he would pick up whatever costs were incurred during your stay."

He thought about Marty. Slowly he began to recall Marty being at his bedside while in the ward.

The nurse looked down at Andrew. "Mr. Simpson, if you're in need of anything while here, press the call button pinned to your pillow. Someone will be in to see to your needs."

"Thank you," he replied.

As the nurse was about to leave the room, she paused at the door and turned toward him. "Oh, by the way, there will be a Dr. Thomason coming see you later today."

She closed the door, leaving Andrew to his private world.

"Who's Dr. Thomason?" he asked aloud.

Andrew looked around the room. Noticing a remote control on the night stand beside his bed, he reached over, grabbed it, wondering what it was for. He held it in his hand and inspected the device. He pushed the ON button.

Instantly the TV monitor mounted on a wall bracket in the corner of the room came to life. He pushed the OFF and ON button. He was amazed, having never used a remote control. Pushing the channel buttons, he stopped at a channel that seemed to be broadcasting something of interest.

Repositioning himself, he became engrossed in a program currently being shown. Although the program turned out to be boring, he continued to watch in an attempt to keep his mind occupied.

Half an hour passed when the door to his room opened again. A tall, distinguished looking man with short black hair with streaks of gray in it, wearing a suit entered the room. He had a stethoscope draped around his neck.

Andrew cautiously looked at him.

"Good morning," The stranger greeted. "I'm Dr. Thomason. How do you feel?"

"A little hazy but otherwise fine," Andrew replied.

"Good!" Dr. Thomason said, appearing to be half listening as he picked up the chart hung on the foot of the bed.

The doctor paged through the chart, reading the various notations that had been entered, and then made his own notations. He returned it to the foot of the bed then contemplated Andrew for a few minutes. Andrew felt uncomfortable. Dr. Thomason broke the silence.

"Andrew, you're an alcoholic. I'm here to get you help with your affliction."

Andrews face reddened.

"First things first," Dr. Thomason said after a short pause. "We took some blood samples to see why you have an elevated high white blood cell count and will have to do some other tests to find out why. After were finished, then we'll take care of that habit of yours. The most important issue is, you must want to free yourself of this affliction, otherwise all I do for you, as well as what others will for you, will be in vain. Do you want to beat this alcoholism?"

"Yes. Yes, I do," Andrew replied, in a sincere voice.

"Good. That's the first step and perhaps the most important. I realize you've had a traumatic experience, so let us take care of the wound of yours first. After you out of danger from the wound, we'll move into the phase of treating your alcoholism. We'll keep you on this pain medication and give you other medications for a few days that will help your body overcome the lack of alcohol in your system. In time these medications will have to go. This is when things may get a little rough for you."

Andrew stirred nervously. He knew being deprived of alcohol would be a battle to the finish, and already the thought of going without began to plague his mind, even though his body was not responding to not having any since he entered the hospital.

"Will I have to stay in this hospital?" Andrew asked.

"No. We'll move you to a rehabilitation center. There you'll be with other patients going through similar programs as yourself."

"What will happen there? Will I be a prisoner? Will it be like this hospital?"

"Andrew, the rehabilitation center is not a prison. You can leave anytime you want, but we would rather you stay. The program will consist of medication, group therapy and individual counseling with one of the staff members. After a few weeks, you'll leave the center, coming back occasionally to get additional support and strength against the disease. Everything will be fine. Just give it a chance."

Dr. Thomason picked his hand and patted it to give him some assurance.

He looked at his watch. "Well, I've got to go. I have other patients to tend to. You just rest. We'll beat your addiction one step at a time."

Dr. Thomason departed the room leaving Andrew to his own thoughts.

Picking up the bed positioning control, Andrew brought the head of the bed up to a semi-setting position. He stared at the TV although not aware of what he was watching.

Andrews stay in the hospital lasted several days. He underwent scores of medical tests. It seemed as though his room was grand central station by the volume of nurses, medical and laboratory technicians parading in and out of his room. As rapidly as the parade of people coming into his started, the activity ceased just as quickly.

By the time he was discharged, the knife wound had healed to a point where there was only the need of a small bandage.

Although he enjoyed the attention he was getting, he was glad to be free from the hospital. He did not like the confinement.

For the first time since he could remember, he actually felt good. The only discomfort was a slight pain in his lower back, which had plagued him for the past few years. He chose to ignore the pain, feeling it was due to his age and the abuse he had given his body over the years. He was elated over how he felt. To his amazement, the need or desire for alcohol did not plague him.

Andrew sat in the hospital lobby, patiently waiting for Marty to arrive. He was wearing a blue checkered flannel shirt, black dress pants and a pair of new loafers Marty had brought to the hospital. Unlike the clothes Marty had given him before, the new clothes made him blend in with those around him. He was clean shaven and looked much younger. He did not look like the haggard derelict of a few days earlier.

Marty walked through the waiting room glass doors. Andrew stood up, eager to see Marty.

"Mr. Fieldman," he said excitedly, "I'm here."

Marty walked up to him. "Well! I must say, you actually are looking good. How do you feel?"

"I feel fine Mr. Fieldman."

"That's good. Just stay put for a moment while I tend to the hospital bill."

Andrew sat back down on the waiting room bench, as Marty disappeared down one of the many corridors to the business office.

An hour passed before Marty was to return. He had a concerned look on his face as he walked toward Andrew.

"Is there anything wrong, Mr. Fieldman?" Andrew asked, as Marty reached him.

"Oh nothing," he said, appearing preoccupied. He changed his expression as he looked down at Andrew.

"Well, that takes care of that," he said. "You ready to go?"

"Yes. I'm ready," Andrew gleefully replied.

The two walked out of the hospital lobby. It was a bright, sunny day. Andrew was elated.

People passed the two going about their business. Euphoric over the attention given him the past few days, as a stranger passed, Andrew suddenly greeted the stranger. "Good morning."

The stranger greeted him with the same replay, smiling at him as he did. Andrew wanted to shout with joy, realizing people responded to him, no longer looking down at him. Marty was amused. He smiled as they walked toward a car.

Reaching the car, Marty unlocked the doors with his remote. He opened the passenger door for Andrew.

"Get in," he said, as he walked around to the driver's side.

Andrew looked at the BMW, asking, "Where's the truck?"

Marty did not hear the question. Andrew opened the door and sat down. Marty opened the driver's side door and got into the car.

"Better put that safety belt on," he said, as he buckled up.

Andrew took the belt in hand but was not sure what to do with it. Marty reached over and buckled the seat belt for him.

"Haven't been in a car lately, have you?"

"No!" replied Andrew.

Marty started the car and drove away from the hospital. Andrew turned and looked back, staring at it until it was out of sight. The two sat in silence as Marty maneuvered through traffic.

Marty appeared to be in deep thought, while they traveled onward. Andrew looked at him, searching for an expression. There was none to be seen. He wanted to talk, to know what was to happen, but was hesitant in asking.

Marty turned the car into a driveway. As he headed toward a colonial looking building, they passed immaculately kept lawns, doted by occasional flower beds equally maintained. Andrew was amazed at the sight.

"What's this place?" Andrew asked as Marty continued up the winding driveway.

"This is the rehabilitation center. You're going to stay here for a few weeks," Marty replied.

Andrew didn't know how to react. It had been a long time since he had seen such beauty. From the sights unfolding before him, it was as though he was in another world. He could not imagine such a place existing and that it would be his temporary residence.

Marty stopped in front of the building. Andrew had expected to see something resembling a hospital, but instead, he was pleasantly surprised that the center looked more like a hotel. A man wearing a white smock stepped up to the car and opened the door to the passengers' side. Andrew looked up, unlatched the seat belt and got out. Marty got out of the car and walked to where Andrew was standing.

"Good morning," the man wearing the white smock greeted. "I'm Jerry Edwards, house attendant. Do you have any luggage?"

"No luggage," replied Marty. "I'll be bringing some things later on."

"Yes, sir," the attendant said. "If you'll follow me, I'll take you to the registration desk."

Marty and Andrew followed the attendant up the walkway and into the lobby of the center. Marty had Andrew sit in a large overstuffed chair in the lobby, and then accompanied the attendant to the registration desk. Once there, Marty busied himself with the necessary papers to have Andrew admitted as a patient.

Andrew scanned the lobby. Except for an occasional staff member wearing white smocks, there was no evidence it was a rehabilitation center. He began to feel at ease as those who would pass by him greeted him with a smile. Everyone seemed so friendly. His unfound fears about being placed in a rehabilitation center vanished.

Marty continued filling out the registration forms. Occasionally he would turn and point toward Andrew when a question was asked. Having finished providing the necessary information, he took several of the forms in hand and walked to Andrew was sitting.

"Here," he said when he reached him, "you'll have to sign these forms before your treatment can begin."

Marty handed him a pen. Andrew carefully signed each form on a line that had been marked with an X by the registration clerk. Marty took the signed documents and returned to the registration desk.

The admissions clerk withdrew a new manila folder and wrote Andrews name on the index tab. Opening the folder, she placed all the papers into it.

"If you'll wait in the lobby, one of our staff members will be here shortly," she said.

Marty returned to Andrew and sat on a chair next to him. "Okay, everything's set," he said. "Your treatment will start today. How do you feel?"

"A little nervous," Andrew replied.

"You'll get over that. These people will give you the best of care."

Andrew half smiled. The two sat in silence as they watched the activity within the lobby.

Several minutes passed when a young woman wearing a white smock stepped up to the registration desk. After a short conversation with the clerk, she turned and walked toward Andrew and Marty. They stood up as she approached them.

"Good morning. I'm Doctor Maxwell," she said, as she looked at Andrew, then at Marty. Marty watched Andrew intently when the doctor greeted them.

A surprised look came to Andrew's face when she drew nearer to them. He studied her carefully, looking into her hazel green eyes. Her long, blonde hair cascaded over her shoulders, shining as though it were pure silk. She appeared uncomfortable as she noticed Andrew studying her every feature. He could not take his eyes off her.

"It can't be," Andrew said, finally breaking the silence.

Marty tugged at Andrew's shirt sleeve in an attempt to distract him. "Andrew, you're embarrassing the doctor," he said.

"It can't be," Andrew said again, continuing to stare at Andrea.

"It can't be what?" questioned Andrea, as she stepped back.

"Oh . . . I'm sorry," Andrew said. "I didn't mean to stare at you. It's just you look like . . . remind me . . . of someone I knew a long time ago."

Andrea brushed a wisp of hair away from her forehead. "I'm sure you must be thinking of someone else," she said. "I don't believe we've ever met. That is to say, I've never met anyone named Andrew Simpson."

Andrea turned toward Marty, noticing his severely scarred face. She extended her hand.

"You must be Mr. Fieldman."

"Yes. Marty Fieldman."

"I'm pleased to meet you. Admissions told me you are sponsoring Mr. Simpson."

"Yes An . . . doctor," he said, almost calling her by her first name."

Andrea looked at Marty questioningly. "We need more people like you," she said. "It's a wonderful what you're doing for Mr. Simpson."

Marty took Andrea's hand and shook it. He held onto her hand longer then one would when greeting.

"Mr. Fieldman?" she said, pulling her hand away.

"Yes. Sorry," he said, as he let go of her hand. "Andrew needs all the help you can give. I'm told this center does wonders for people with addiction similar to Mr. Simpson's."

"We try," Andrea replied. "In reality, it's the patient who cures themselves of their affliction, not us. We only provide the support and counseling needed to help them rid themselves of the habit. Only if the patient is willing to be cured will we be able to succeed."

Andrew watched the doctors every move as the two talked. He could not keep his eyes off of Andrea. His thoughts took him back to a time long, long ago. Without giving it a thought, Andrew extended his hand toward the doctor. Andrea turned toward him and extended her hand.

As their hands touched, she felt a tingling sensation. Andrea seemed at a loss for words. Andrew held onto her hand as though meeting a long lost friend.

The silence was broken by the appearance of an orderly.

"Mr. Simpson?" the orderly questioned, as he approached, looking at Marty, then Andrew.

"Yes," Andrew replied, turning to the orderly, as he let go of Andreas' hand.

"I'm here to show you to your room. Are you ready?"

"Yes," he replied.

"Please follow me," the orderly instructed.

Andrew turned toward Marty. "Thank you," he said, and then glanced at Andrea. "Will I see you again?"

"Yes," Andrea assured. "I'll be one of your attending doctors."

Marty stood up. "I must be going now," he said.

Andrea thanked him again for his support of Andrew. Marty walked through the lobby and exited out the front door.

Andrew followed the orderly. He continued looking at the doctor as he walked away from her, turning occasionally to see where was going. He was barely conscience of his surroundings as he made his way through the rehabilitation center. His thoughts were interrupted when they reached a door on the second floor of the center.

"This will be your room during your stay here," the orderly said, as he opened the door to the room. As they entered the room, the orderly took a plastic band out of his pocket.

"I need to put this identification band on your wrist so we can identify you for the administration of medication."

Andrew held out his arm for the orderly to place the band on it, while surveying the room. He was pleasantly surprised at how the room was decorated. It looked much like one would find in a hotel. It had a single bed, dresser, desk, a comfortable cloth covered chair, a small refrigerator and curtains covering the windows. Another door in the room led to a small bathroom. He was delighted knowing he would not have to share his room with another patient.

"Lunch will be served at eleven thirty," the orderly said, as Andrew viewed his new surroundings. "I'll come and get you when it's time for you to eat."

"Thank you," Andrew said, appearing preoccupied with other thoughts.

The orderly closed the door, leaving Andrew alone. He walked over to the bed and sat down on it. Feeling sleepy, he laid down. Closing his eyes, he fell into a twilight sleep, dreaming of the past. For the first time since he could remember while asleep, Claire entered his mind.

Andrew tossed and turned as he dreamed of Claire. In his minds eye, a distorted face would fade between Claire and Andrea.

"Claire!" he cried out.

The sound of his voice echoed throughout the room, only to be absorbed by his surroundings.

Suddenly a knock came on the door.

"Mr. Simpson," a voice called out. "I'm here to take you to lunch."

With a start, Andrew awoke. His face was wet with sweat. He remained on the bed a moment to collect his thoughts.

"Mr. Simpson," the voice called again. "Are you up? Lunch is ready. I'll wait out here until you're ready to go."

He sat up in the bed. "Yes. Just give me a moment," he called out."

Getting up, he walked to the bathroom. Reaching a sink, he turned on the faucet and splashed some water on his face. He looked into the mirror.

"Is she, Claire?" he murmured an enigmatic question.

CHAPTER SEVEN

HE QUICKLY DRIED his face, walked to the door and opened it. The orderly who had previously escorted him to his room stood in the corridor.

"Lunch, Mr. Simpson. Are you ready?"

"Yes," Andrew replied.

Preoccupied, Andrew followed the orderly as the two walked to the dining room. The long rectangular room was walled with oak wood, accented by sconce lights on either side of its length. The windows on one side of the room looked out to a garden featuring statues, flowers and a decorative pool fed by a stone water fall. Rows of evenly spaced poplar trees hid the area from the view of others.

The orderly positioned Andrew at a pre-selected chair. Andrew sat down and waited.

Several moments passed as other residents of the center began entering the dining room. When everybody was seated, dining room attendants began to bring food out of the kitchen, placing platters on the tables, much like a boarding house. The residents in turn, filled their plates. Andrew followed, filling his plate. Little was spoken as they ate.

Sitting across the table opposite Andrew was a young man who appeared to be in his late twenties. He was impeccably groomed and was dressed in clothes that would indicate he was of wealth.

Toward the end of the meal he looked over at Andrew.

"You're new here. I'm an alcoholic," he said. "What's your problem? What kind of addiction do you have?"

Andrew flinched. He did not want to answer. "I'm a . . ." he paused.

"You're a what?" the young man demanded.

"I'm a . . ." Andrew did could not bring himself to admit his downfall. It embarrassed him too much to talk about it, especially to a complete stranger.

"Are you an alcoholic, a drug user?" questioned the young man.

Andrews face became flush. "I'm not a drug user," he blurted, his face reddening even more.

The residents around the table looked at Andrew, each giving him their full attention. No one spoke further. He was uncomfortable with everyone staring at him.

"Go ahead. Say it," the young man said loudly. "You're an alcoholic, aren't you?"

"Yes, I'm an alcoholic," Andrew said in a low voice, lowering his head as he spoke.

The young man laughed as the other occupants of the room clapped at his revelation. He looked up in surprise, glancing around the table at each person. They were all smiling at him.

"That's the first step toward your cure," the young man said. "Admitting to us and yourself you're addicted to alcohol."

Each resident introduced themselves to Andrew and in turn told of their downfall in life. By the time each had spoken, Andrew began to feel relaxed. He realized he was not the only one in the world with a problem in life that seemed incurable.

The group continued making small talk to one another. Andrew said little, watching carefully as they each carried on conversations with one another.

The meal finished, each resident filed out of the dining room, leaving Andrew to sit alone. He was not sure of what to do next. Attendants came into the dining room and set about cleaning the table of the dishes, eating utensils and linens. An attendant looked at Andrew.

"Sir, if you don't have a session, you're free to go back to your room, the library or activity room if you wish."

"Thank you," he acknowledged, then got up and departed the dining hall, returning to his room. As he opened the door, he noticed there was no lock and the handle was very similar to a door one would find in a hospital room.

Andrew walked to the window and glanced outside. He stood watching people milling about the grounds. He wondered what was in store for him. The door to his room opened. A nurse stepped inside the room.

"Mr. Simpson?"

Andrew turned away from the window. "Yes?" he answered.

The nurse was holding a small tray with several small paper cups on it. He set the tray on the credenza against the wall opposite the foot of the bed.

"May I see your name tag please?"

"Name tag?" Andrew asked.

"Yes, the name tag on your wrist."

Andrew looked down at his wrist at the tag placed there earlier. He raised his hand for the nurse to see.

The nurse looked at the printing on the tag. "Okay, this medication is for you."

The nurse handed Andrew a cup containing several pills.

"Here. Take these please," the nurse instructed. She opened the small refrigerator and withdrew a bottle of water, removed the cap and handed it to Andrew.

Andrew took the bottled water. He looked into the cup containing several small pills. As instructed, he placed the pills into his mouth and swallowed them along with the water the nurse had handed him.

"What are these for?" he asked, after taking the pills.

"I don't know," the nurse replied. "You'll have to ask the doctor. You have a session later today. Someone will come to get you."

The nurse quickly departed the room, leaving Andrew alone. He returned to the window and continued watching the activity outside.

Several minutes passed, when he began to feel slightly hazy. Surmising he was feeling the effects of the medication given him, he decided to lie on the bed. Once again he fell into a peaceful sleep.

He was asleep half an hour, when the door to his room partially opened. A woman, without stepping into the room looked down at him lying on the bed.

"No," she said, in an exasperated voice. "I can't believe it's you after all these years. Why did you have to come back?"

She stood a few moments staring at Andrew. She wanted to walk over to the bed to get a better look at him, but hesitated in doing so. Several moments passed, when someone tapped her on the shoulder.

"Mother!" Andrea exclaimed. "What are you doing?"

She quickly closed the door, turning toward Andrea. Except for her hair being cut short and the need for glasses, the two could almost pass as sisters. Although in her late forties, Claire retained her youthful looks and slim figure.

"Oh, I thought I heard this patient cry out and decided to take a look inside. I was sure he was under some sort of stress and needed help."

"Hardly mother," Andrea replied. "Mr. Simpson is under sedation. You are well aware this is one of our first steps in weaning alcoholic patients him from their affliction. It's to help prevent the onslaught of the DT's. You know as much."

"Mr. Simpson," she said, "Isn't he the patient who was admitted earlier this morning?"

"Yes, mother," Andrea replied.

Andrea continued watching her mother, sensing there was something on her mind.

"What's the matter? You seem preoccupied with the patient. What is it?"

"No! No!" she replied. "You know me Andrea. I'm somewhat fastidious when it comes to our patients."

"Yes, I know you are but this is just another patient."

"Yes," she said, stretching the word out as though in deep thought. "Was he a self admitted patient?"

Andrea looked down at the clipboard she was carrying.

"No. He was brought in by a Mr. Fieldman. In fact, he's sponsoring him, picking up all his expenses."

The woman gasped at Andrea's reply. "Mr. Fieldman?"

"Yes."

"Marty Fieldman?"

"As a matter of fact, it is a Marty Fieldman. Why do you ask? Do you know him?"

"Yes! . . ." She paused. "Yes. I believe I met him once before. He likes helping people. A real nice person!" She cut her answer short to avoid any further questioning from Andrea.

"Okay mom," Andrea said. "With our expert care and the help of Mr. Fieldman, we'll get this patient back on his feet."

Andrea's mother looked into her eyes. "Be careful, darling," she said, then turned and walked away.

Andrea stood watching as her mother departed. "What do you mean by that comment?" Andrea called out as her mother disappeared around a corridor. "I'm always careful."

Andrea put the incident out of her mind. She looked down at her clipboard, made a notation, turned and walked down the hall to tend to a patient listed on her schedule.

CHAPTER EIGHT

MARTY RETURNED TO the rehabilitation center with several boxes, stopping at the reception desk.

"I brought some clothes for Mr. Simpson," he said.

"Just leave them here, Mr. Fieldman," the receptionist said. "I'll have an orderly take them to his room."

"Thank you," he replied. He was about to leave when Claire who had just entered the lobby approached him.

"Marty. How could you do such a thing?" she whispered.

Marty turned around.

"Well! If it isn't Claire Maxwell," he said sarcastically. "So, we're on speaking terms now doctor and after all these years of silence. Why the sudden interest?" he asked.

"You know what it's all about. You're creating a big problem for me. I don't particularly appreciate what you're doing. You can ruin all I've done for Andrea. Why did you have to bring him here? There are other centers you could have easily taken him to for treatment."

"Why not here? This is a rehabilitation center, isn't it?" Marty snapped back.

Claire flinched, as she looked around the lobby. Several people within earshot began looking at the two as they spoke.

"Do we have to talk about this in the lobby?" she quickly whispered. "People are beginning to look at us. Besides, Andrea is liable to appear and see we are having a confrontation. I don't want her to see me talking with you while I'm distraught."

Marty's face flushed. He motioned toward the main entrance.

The two walked to the lobby doors and stepped outside. As the doors closed behind them, they continued walking further down the sidewalk.

"Why did you have to bring Andrew to my clinic?" she questioned.

"Because Andrew needs help Claire. He's an alcoholic. You do help people overcome various addictions, don't you?"

"Yes Marty, but Andrew here?" she emphasized. "What if he should run into me? What can I say after all these years? What am I to do? Please understand, all I'm trying to do is protect Andrea. It would be devastating to her if she knew about him. You shouldn't have brought Andrew here."

"You won't relent, will you?" Marty retorted. "You live in this perfect world, your own shell. You refuse to recognize the slightest problem, the merest imperfection people have. Well, unfortunately, life isn't perfect and it's high time you realize it isn't the world you'd like it to be."

"He left, Marty. He just dropped out," Claire argued. "What did you expect me to do?"

"It was the chemical. You damn well remember, don't you?"

Claire closed her eyes. She did not want to rehash what had happened so long ago.

Marty watched as Claire paused, recalling her past while Andrew was married to her. She knew Andrew had a problem working for the government in the development of a secret defoliant. She would plead and beg him to slow down on his alcohol consumption. It was to no avail. One day Andrew didn't come home. He dropped out of society, lost his job, vanishing to be swallowed up among the multitude of street nomads.

"I was pregnant when he left, Marty," Claire finally said. "He doesn't even know about Andrea."

"So you acquired a divorce and went back to using your maiden name. You even gave Andrea your maiden name, just so he couldn't find you if he decided to come back. How could you harbor such hate?"

Claire gave Marty curt look.

"Hate? I don't hate him. I never did. I just had to get on with my life without him."

"Do you still love him?" Marty questioned.

Claire did not respond.

"You know," Marty commented after several moments of silence, "you could have worked things out with him. He was under severe stress. You know he didn't like what he was developing at the lab."

"He couldn't cope," Claire said defensively. "He was going downhill fast and shut up like a clam, refusing to talk to me or anyone else."

"That's a poor excuse. You knew he was fighting with himself, knowing he was instrumental in the development of that secret defoliant. He was aware of what it would do to humans, warning anyone that would listen. When he learned the chemical was going to be used in Vietnam, it was the straw that broke the camel's back."

"It was more than that," Claire snapped. "Our marriage was deteriorating. The honeymoon was over. It was a time of constant bickering, fighting and him drinking himself into a stupor every night. If he didn't leave, then I would have. You're being a little hard on me, Marty. How can you expect anyone to live under the circumstances that existed with him back then?"

Marty looked at Claire. He could see she was distraught. He turned toward her and put his hands on her shoulders.

"What's done is done Claire. There's no way we can undo what has happened and it's pointless to drag up the past. We have to look toward the future. If Andrew comes out of this thing, he may decide to look you up. What will you do then?"

"Yes. With your help I suppose," Claire managed to say as the tears welled up in her eyes.

Marty waited until Claire regained her composure. She looked at him and smiled.

"There were some good times, you know. I really loved the good times we had. We were in love, Andrew and me. If only he would have opened up to me. Maybe we could have worked things out."

"Maybe?" Marty said. "You pushed too hard, Claire. Just like you pushed Andrea. You have a knack of causing events to go your way. You even maneuvered your parents against me because of Elizabeth."

"Why not? If it wasn't for me, Andrea wouldn't be a doctor today. Sure I pushed. I wanted the best for her."

"Even if it means hurting people you love, your own relations?"

Claire turned her face away. "That's a cruel thing to say."

Marty took his hands off her shoulders.

"Look Claire, let's not argue. I still hold you dear to me. You're the only link I have with Elizabeth. Believe me; I've suffered plenty because of the accident. I'm only here because of Andrew."

"Then you knew this was my clinic?" Claire asked.

"Yes. I've known for many years."

"What about Andrea? Did you know she was here too?"

"Yes. I followed her development throughout her life. Some of the people you know, well, I also know. Besides, Andrea is my niece regardless of what happened in the past."

"Who? Who do you know?"

"It's not important. Just remember I kept my distance, knowing how you felt about me. I didn't want to upset your precious world. Besides the time wasn't right to come to you and ask for forgiveness for what happened to your sister. Now the time is here."

"Why? Because of Andrew?"

"Partly," Marty said. "It's a little deeper then just him being a patient."

Claire looked at Marty abruptly. "Where did you find him? How did you find him?"

Marty hesitated.

"Tell me, Marty. How did you find him? How much have you told him?"

Marty looked down at the ground.

"He's been coming to my scrap yard for some time, but I wasn't aware of it. When I finally met him, I was shocked at the state he was in. I didn't tell him anything. He doesn't know you work here or that he has a daughter."

"You've had contact with him for some time and said nothing to me?"

"Now hold on," Marty said, raising his voice. "Remember, we were not on speaking terms. I didn't see you making any effort to come to the scrap yard, much less try to locate Andrew. Anyway, I didn't know he was coming there. It was by chance I found out about him."

Claire looked away. "What business would I have in a scrap yard?"

"Me. You know I was devoted to Elizabeth. A little consideration on your part would have helped. You could have made an effort to contact me, even saw fit to forgive me. No, I suppose you're still begrudging me for Elizabeth's death."

Claire gave Marty a sharp look.

"Sorry," Marty said, smiling wryly. "I'll leave it alone. Andrew would come to the yard several times a week to sell whatever scrap metal he could find. I imagine the little cash he got kept him in alcohol."

Claire put her hands to her face. "How horrible! What a terrible way to live. What did you do when you found out he was Andrew?"

"I wasn't sure it was him at first, but seeing a picture of you he was carrying, I knew it was Andrew. I was shocked to see his state of deterioration. I asked him if he wanted to work for me. I couldn't just stand by, doing nothing, knowing who he was."

"Are you sure you didn't tell him about Andrea?"

"No. I told you as much. Besides, I don't know how to handle the situation. I feel it best to leave that up to you. It's cruel, Claire. It's cruel for a man not knowing he has a child."

"You're leaving it up to me? What am I supposed to do? Wave a magic wand and everything will be perfect?"

"You know you can do something about this situation if you want. The question is do you want to? Will you?" he admonished.

Claire avoided Marty's eyes. She was at a loss for a reply.

"He was in a hospital before coming here. How did Andrew end up in the hospital?" she asked, attempting to change the subject.

"He was attacked while staying in a hotel room a week ago and ended up in the county hospital emergency room. While there, I arranged for Doctor Thomason to stop in to see him. With a little persuasion by me and the doctor, we got him, with his approval, admitted to your rehabilitation center."

"You know Dr. Thomason?"

"Yes. We've known each other for years. He happens to be my nephew, my sister's son. What does that matter?"

Claire looked at Marty suspiciously. She asked, "You mean Andrew actually volunteered to go though the treatment. To be cured of his addiction?"

"Yes. Hopefully he'll be cured, if everyone involved gives him the help he needs. Besides, this is for his sake as well as Andreas."

Claire did not say anything. She gazed across the snow covered lawn toward the distant trees. Her thoughts were in a turmoil.

"Marty, I'm not sure I can do this," she said. "I don't want Andrea upset. It would be too great a shock, finding out her father is alive, especially after I told her he was killed. I just can't do it."

"Claire," Marty interrupted. "It must be done. You have to tell him about Andrea. Andrew may not have much time left."

"What do you mean?" she asked.

Marty's face became saddened. "He's very ill. He may be dying, Claire."

"My God! Are you sure, Martin? What's wrong with him?"

Marty hesitated, as though preoccupied, reviewing what he had learned about Andrew.

"Well, it seems all those years of drinking have caught up with him. He has sclerosis of the liver. I found out when he was in the hospital. Concerned about his elevated white blood cell count, Doctor Thomason had tests run. He told me his disease could be terminal but won't know until all the tests are in. Andrew doesn't know."

Claire looked away from Marty. She did not say anything more. She began to walk across the lawn toward a bench located in a garden alcove. Marty followed. Reaching the bench, Claire sat down. Marty stood a few steps away watching her every move and expression. Looking across the lawn, she glanced, at the planted chrysanthemums in the flower bed, covered with a light dusting of snow.

"What beautiful flower," she finally said, "and for such a short time. They're my favorite, especially the yellow ones."

"The color of friendship!" Marty said.

She knew the meaning of what Marty had intoned. Not responding, she continued to look at the flowers.

"It's too soon, Marty. It's just too soon. I'm not ready for this."

"We're never ready, Claire. Life throws us some pretty hard curves. You just have to cope. You just have to pick yourself up and continue on with your life. You owe this to Andrew and Andrea."

"Like Andrew? He didn't cope. Why all of a sudden must I? I don't feel I owe him anything."

"Let's not analyze again, Claire. Can't you give in? What's it going to take to break through that shell of yours?"

Claire peered at Marty. "The shell is to protect me from the things in life I dislike. Besides, I don't have to take this."

She got up and began walking.

"Claire!" Marty called.

She ignored Marty's outcry and continued walking toward the entrance to the center. Marty watched as she made her way to the front door. He shook his head in disbelief.

"How am I going to get through to her?" he said to himself, as she disappeared into the interior of the building.

Claire walked swiftly, keeping her head down. She did not want anyone to see her in tears. Reaching the main entrance, she opened one of the glass doors, stepped inside and walked through the lobby toward the ladies room. Without noticing, she passed Andrea, who was about to say something. Andrea called after her but she did not acknowledge her.

Andrea walked to the ladies room door, opened it and stepped inside. Claire stood in front of a mirror above one of the sinks, blotting her tear stained face.

"Mother!" Andrea said, as the door closed behind her. "What's the matter? Why are you crying?"

Claire glanced around the room to see if anyone else was present. Assured the two were the only occupants of the room, she turned toward Andrea. She put her hand to Andrea's head, brushing a strand of hair out of her eyes.

"You're such a beautiful girl," she said.

Andrea caught hold of her mother's hand. "What's wrong? You've been crying."

She let go of her hand as Claire turned toward the mirror, looking at her reflection.

Andrea waited patiently, knowing her mother would eventually tell her what was bothering her.

Claire was a proud person, proper in her demeanor and always on top of any situation she encountered, however, Marty presented a quagmire to her, and she wasn't sure how she was going to handle it.

She felt uncomfortable being in the ladies room, having to reveal to her daughter something she had been keeping from her since her birth.

"Not here. Let's go to your office."

Andrea nodded. The two walked out of the ladies room toward Andrea's office, saying nothing to one another as they walked through the center.

Reaching the office, Andrea opened the door, letting her mother step inside. Claire stood in the room surveying the surroundings.

The room was full of expensive antique statues, vases and paintings, lighted by down lights placed strategically to accent them. The oak covered walls tempered the room, making it comfortable for anyone entering. Andrea's diplomas from the various universities adorned the walls. It appeared more a den one would retire for relaxation than an office. Removing her coat, she sat down.

"I'm so proud of you, darling," Claire said. "It would hurt me deeply if anything or anyone ruined your success."

Andrea looked at her mother in surprise.

"Now, what is that supposed to mean? What could or who could ruin what I've worked for all these years? Besides, you're evading the issue. What's bothering you?"

Claire sighed. "I imagine you'll eventually find out."

"Find out what, mother?"

Claire held back in answering for a few minutes. She was fearful of her daughters' reaction.

"Mother!" Andrea exclaimed. "Find out what?"

Claire appeared distraught. Sensing her un-comfort Andrea walked to the chair, stooped down and put her arm around her mother's neck. Claire put her arms around her daughter tightly.

"Mother," Andrea whispered, "it can't be that bad."

Claire looked into Andrea's eyes.

"Sit down, darling. I have something to tell you that you may find disturbing."

Andrea withdrew her arms from around her mother, walked over to a sofa and sat down with a puzzled expression on her face.

"Believe me darling, what I have to tell you, I didn't mean to keep from you. Throughout the years, I wanted to protect you so nothing would happen to you while you were growing up, so I kept certain pieces of information from you."

Claire began fidgeting, wringing her hands. Andrea had never seen her mother so at unease.

"Mother," Andrea broke in, trying to ease the tension, "I'm a big girl now. I'm sure I can handle anything you have to tell me. You taught me to stand up to the worst that can happen. What are you afraid to tell me?"

Claire sighed. "It's my sister. I had a sister."

Andrea's mouth opened at the sudden revelation. "I have an aunt and you never told me? Why? Where is she? When can I meet her?"

she asked excitedly, and then realizing what her mother had said questioned, "Had?"

Claire turned away from Andrea, not wanting to reveal the hurt she was feeling.

Andrea reiterated. "Mother? What are you saying? What do you mean had?"

Claire turned and looked at Andrea.

"Darling, it was so long ago. It wouldn't have mattered if you had known about her. She died before you were born. It's in the past. The present is what counts."

"I don't think knowing I had an aunt would have made any difference unless she was some sort of embarrassment to the family. What was her name? What was she like?"

Claire felt relieved seeing Andrea was rational about the news.

"Her name was Elizabeth," she said calmly.

"What a beautiful name, Elizabeth," Andrea said. "What was she like? What happened to her?"

"She was beautiful, like you," Claire answered. "We were very close. We did everything together. People thought we were twins because we looked so much alike, even though we were a year apart. You wouldn't find one of us without the other close behind. We shared our deepest secrets, wishes, everything. You would have loved her."

"Why is it grandmother and grandfather didn't say anything about her?"

"It was because of our loss! You see darling, we all were very close. Elizabeth's death left a deep wound in us. To keep the hurt away, we blocked her death from our minds. It was a lot to bear. You could never know the closeness of sisters unless you had one."

Andrea could hear the pain in her mother's voice. She let the conversation come to a lull.

Claire withdrew a tissue from her purse and patted the tears that were forming in her eyes.

"Enough of that," she said, smiling at Andrea.

Andrea smiled back. "Alright, mother. I am disappointed you didn't tell me but I'll get over not knowing I had an aunt. I'm just sorry you had to bear this pain by yourself all these years knowing my father was killed before I was born. Don't you think it would have been easier had I know about your sister?"

Claire looked away. "I suppose, darling. I didn't want anything to ruin your life. It was my sorrow, not yours."

"How could your sorrow hurt me?" Andrea asked.

Claire paused. She closed her eyes, fearful of what she was about to say. Carefully selecting her words, she continued.

"There's more, Andrea. You see, it was the times. It was the sixties, with free love, the Vietnam War, protesters, people wanting to do their own thing. Your aunt Elizabeth got caught up in the movement. In fact, I too got caught up in the times but I was a little more rational than Elizabeth."

"Did drugs kill her?" Andrea asked.

"No. Thank God she had sense enough to keep away from drugs. She was killed in an automobile accident, by a drunk driver."

Andrea cringed. Working at the rehabilitation center, she was all too familiar with patients responsible for the deaths of others due to alcohol.

"She was only seventeen at the time. She was mar . . ." Claire stopped short.

Andrea looked at her in sudden surprise. "What were you about to say? She was married?"

Claire looked away from her. "Yes! She was married," came her reluctant reply. "In a sense that is. They weren't even together a year. She ran around with him, dressed like a hippie, expressing free love, a flower child. I tried countless times to warn her, to tell her she needed to come down to earth, to reality. As close as we were, she wouldn't listen to me."

"Then I have an uncle," Andrea said solemnly.

Claire looked at Andrea. "I'm not really sure. Possibility, I guess because of the common-law marriage between Elizabeth and her boyfriend, you could consider him an uncle."

"Am I an aunt, with nephews and nieces? Did they have any children?" Andrea asked eagerly.

"No which was a blessing. Who knows how the children would turn out."

"Mother!" exclaimed Andrea. "What a horrible thing to say."

Claire smiled wryly. "I suppose it was for the best. We, that is, my parents or me would have had to raise the children."

"So, my aunt Elizabeth and her common-law husband were killed in an automobile accident," Andrea surmised.

"No. He wasn't killed," Claire replied. "The fact is, he was the dunk driver responsible for the accident. She was only seventeen years old at the time."

Andrea sat with her mouth agape. "What? He's still alive? Why didn't you tell me? Why have you kept this from me?"

"I was protecting you. Your supposed uncle was responsible for Elizabeth's death. Don't you understand? He was responsible for killing Elizabeth."

"Protecting me from what? If he loved Elizabeth as much as you love me, how can he hurt me?"

Claire was at a loss for an answer.

"Mother, I appreciate you wanting to protect me but I don't see how my uncle, regardless of what he's done in the past, could do me harm."

"He can hurt you. Andrea. Please believe me. He can harm your well being."

"I'm not going to relent. I want to know who my uncle is and why you're so set against me meeting him. Is he a criminal, addict? What?"

Claire turned away from Andrea. She remained silent, holding back, fearing what Marty might have to say to her.

"This is useless Andrea said angrily. "You know I can go to the county and using my aunt's maiden name, find out who my uncle is."

"I doubt you'll be able to finds out about him that way," Claire responded quickly. "They were common-law, never really married as far as I know, so there would be no record of marriage. It was a thing Elizabeth was going through. As I said, she was caught up in the movement of the times, living a careless, reckless life."

Andrea snapped back, "I will find out, Mother! You might as well tell me."

"Leave it be. You're happy, successful. Why dig up the past. Why upset yourself with what's dead and buried? Please, be satisfied with what's happening to you now. You have a brilliant future. Don't let what happened in the past ruin it."

Andrea glared at her mother. From her facial expression, her rage was apparent. "Mother, look at me! I'm going to find out who my uncle is one way or another."

Claire held fast. "It's best for you not to know about him. You can't realize what happened in the past and I'm sure you need not know. There was a lot of pain. Besides, from what I've told you so far and your grandparents being dead, I don't see how you can find out who your uncle is. Why can't you be satisfied with what you've been told so far? Your aunt is dead. I wouldn't have told you as much had I known you would react this way."

Andrea half listened to what her mother was saying. "Mother!" Andrea said, interrupting her, "I need to tend to something. I think it best you leave."

Claire was surprised by the sudden interruption. She got up and walked toward the door. Andrea stood fast, watching as she opened the door, disappearing behind it.

CHAPTER NINE

ANDREA CONTEMPLATED WHAT had just transpired. She was perplexed, not sure of what to do or could do about the matter. The unexpected had been dropped in her lap. She was hurt her mother kept the secret of her aunt and uncle from her. She walked to her desk chair and sat down.

She was in deep thought, when someone knocked on her office door. "Come in," she called out.

The door opened. In stepped a tall, well tanned man. The tailored suite he was wearing accentuated his physique indicating he visited the gym frequently. It was Andrea's fiancée.

"Michael!" she exclaimed.

Andrea got up from the chair and ran to him, putting her arms around him. She buried her head in this chest and began to cry.

"Whoa. What's this?" Michael asked.

Andrea looked into Michael's dark gray eyes. Happy to see him, she managed a smile.

"That's better," he said.

Reaching into his jacket pocket, he took a handkerchief from his pocket and carefully began blotting the tears from her face.

The two stood without saying a word, looking into each other's eyes. Michael drew her closed to him and tenderly kissed her.

"Now," he commended, "tell me what this is all about. What's the matter?"

Andrea began to pace the office floor. "It's my mother."

Michael's expression changed. "Oh her? Now what? What is she meddling in now?"

Andrea knew the two were not fond of one another and her mothers' disapproval of Michael. Her mother would never discuss why she felt this way about Michael. Andrea stopped pacing the floor. Turning, she looked at him.

"My mother had a sister, but she died long ago, before I was born. I don't understand why she has been keeping this information from me. She has her reasons, but what bothers me the most is, I have an uncle who is still alive, or I believe is still alive. My mother was very vague about the issue."

A puzzled look appeared on Michaels face. "That's strange. Your grandparents never mentioned having another daughter. I thought your mother was any only child. So who is this uncle of yours?"

"I don't know," Andrea said. "She won't tell me."

Michael put his hand to his chin.

"She just passed me in the corridor without saying a word, as though preoccupied."

"Guilt, I suppose," Andrea commented. "We had a little falling out. I told her I'd find out who my uncle is, regardless of the consequences. She wasn't happy when she left my office. I will find out, Michael."

"I'm sure you will," mused Michael. "What has me puzzled is how your grandparents and your mother managed to keep this information from me and you all these years. After your grandparents adopted me, they treated me like their own son. He helped me and guided me through college. If it wasn't for them, I wouldn't be editor of the paper."

Andrea smiled and stretched out her arms beckoning him toward her.

"Yes! Despite mother, had it not been for grandfather, I wouldn't have ever met you. Even though you're my uncle, adopted uncle that is," she giggled.

Andrea walked up to Michael. The two embraced again. They kissed and continued holding each other.

"Michael?" Andrea asked, "How can I find out about my uncle? Who he is? Where he is?"

"I suppose," Michael said thoughtfully, "we could hire a private investigator but I really don't want people digging into the Maxwell' past. Besides, if we don't have any information about your uncle, a name, anything, all attempts to locate him will come to a dead end."

The two stood silent, each contemplating the situation.

Suddenly Michael broke the silence. "You said your aunt was dead. How did she die?"

Andrea perked up. "She was killed in an automobile accident, which would have been reported in the newspaper. But where, when? Let's go down to the paper and go through the dead newspaper files."

"Hold on, darling," Michael interjected. "First we need a time period. When did she die? When was the accident?"

"I don't know. Mother didn't say."

"Surely there's a clue. Let's see. How old was she when she died?"

"Mother mentioned she was only seventeen. And her name was Elizabeth, and a year younger than mother."

"Great! A starting point for me. I'll search our archives at the paper."

"Let me go with you. Please," Andrea begged.

"Don't you have patients to look after?"

"Just a minute," Andrea said.

She walked over to her desk, picked up her appointment book and paged through it. She picked up the phone receiver and dialed a few numbers.

"Miss Evert," she said. "Something has come up. Cancel my appointments for today. Doctor Anderson will cover for me should any of my resident patients have an emergency?"

Satisfied with the reply, she put the receiver back onto the cradle, walked over to a closet and withdrew her coat.

"Let's go."

Michael put on his overcoat and the two walked out of the office, down the corridor and headed toward the main entrance. As the two reached the lobby, Andrea noticed Marty standing at the registration desk.

Catching sight of Andrea, Marty called out. "Doctor Maxwell."

Andrea stopped a few steps in front of the door. Marty walked up to her. He glanced at Michael. "How you doing son," he greeted.

A blank expression came over Michaels face. "Fine!" he replied.

"How may I help you? Andrea asked, getting Marty's attention.

"Doctor, I'm Marty Fieldman. Remember? I brought Mr. Simpson in for treatment. Mr. Andrew Simpson. You are his doctor, are you not?

"Yes I am. What can I do for you?"

Marty gazed into Andrea's eyes. He paused for a few seconds before speaking further.

"How is he doing?"

Andrea felt uncomfortable at the way Marty was looking at her. Normally she was able to cope with people but Marty seemed to bother her. Michael stood by, watching without saying a word.

"So far he's doing fine."

Marty smiled. "Good. Is there anything I can do for him, you?"

"No. Everything's fine," Andrea replied. "If you don't mind, I have an important meeting. Will you excuse me please?"

"Yes I understand. If he or you need anything, don't hesitate to contact me."

Andrea did not reply. She turned to Michael and motioned toward the front door. The two left Marty and departed the building.

Marty watched as the two disappeared behind the doors.

"What's bothering you?" Michael asked.

"He gives me the creeps, that Marty fellow. Did you notice how he was looking at me? It was as though he was undressing me or something. And his face! Did you notice all those terrible scares? He has half an ear missing. He looks somewhat sinister, like a gangster or something. And he called you son. God I wouldn't want someone looking like that to be my father."

Michael smiled. "You're imagining things. He's just concerned about a patient. Nothing more and calling me son is just an expression older men use when addressing younger men."

"Why do I feel so strange around him? It's like I should know him, as though I've met him somewhere."

"There you go again, darling. What did I tell you about that psychic business? You and your sixth sense."

"Well, I can't help it. It's just a feeling I get. I even get goose bumps when I'm around certain people. Like that Mr. Fieldman."

Michael laughed as the two continued walking toward the car. Michael unlocked the door and opened it for Andrea. She sat down, giving Michael a sympathetic look. He closed the door, walked to the driver's side and slid onto the seat. Starting the car, he drove off, heading toward the newspaper building.

"Come on, slide over here," he said after they traveled a short distance.

Andrea unbuckled the seat belt and slid next to Michael. He put his arm around her. She put her head on his shoulder.

"Michael!" she asked, "Why don't we just elope. It would be much easier, knowing mother disproves of you."

Michael repositioned himself. "Now, you know that is not practical. What would people say? We're people of stature, looked at by the public. The newspapers would have a field day in the gossip columns. Besides, as reluctant as your mother is about our upcoming wedding, she'd go into a rage if we did elope. No darling, let's do it the proper way."

Andrea kissed Michael on the cheek. "Bummer! I suppose you're right. I just can't wait to have a baby, your baby."

"And what about your career, doctor?"

"That can wait," she replied, whispering into his ear. "I can put that on hold."

"Be sensible. The wedding is only two weeks away."

Andrea sat up and slid back to the passenger's side of the car.

"You're so practical, sometimes too practical. Let's do it. I want you, darling. You know you can have me anytime."

Michael squirmed in his seat. Andrea had the perfect shape, as well as beauty. She was never without a boyfriend as she grew up, often sought after by the most handsome of men. Out of respect and love for her, Michael had vowed he would keep her pure for their wedding night.

Michael's expression changed. "Why does your mother use her maiden name and give you her maiden name when you were born?"

Andrea really had never given it any thought.

"I guess it was because of my father," she replied. "They were married very young but things didn't work out between them. They separated, and then divorced. He joined the Army, and was killed in Vietnam before I was born. She never talks about him. I have no idea what he looked like. I've asked her countless times about him. She said it was a closed subject."

"What was his name?"

"Alex. That's all I know."

"And his last name?"

Andrea's expression became blank. She shrugged her shoulders.

"I don't know. Mother wouldn't tell. Except for her giving birth to me, she said it was not a pleasant time in her life. She reverted back to using her maiden name when they separated."

"You mean there are no pictures of him anywhere in her house?"

"No. That's why I have no idea what he looked like."

"What about your birth certificate? His name would be on it. Why not get a copy? At least you would know his last name."

"No. Mother said she didn't want to go through the pain of remembering him. I'd rather not. It isn't important anyway. He's dead, and besides I don't know where the birth certificate is."

"Why didn't your mother remarry?"

"I really don't know. She was beautiful and had several men who wanted to marry her. She just never remarried."

"Religion? Ethics? Maybe she still loved him?"

"I honestly don't know, Michael. She won't let me bring up the subject, although sometimes she appears melancholy when I try to talk about him. With her being so secretive, it is hard to get into her mind."

"I wonder what she is hiding," Michael commented thoughtfully. "Perhaps looking into the past we will find out what skeletons are buried in her closet."

"Do you think that would be a good idea?" she asked nervously. "I don't want to upset mother."

"Why not? Would you not want to know about your father? At least know what he looked like?"

Andrea felt even more apprehensive. "Yes. But I don't want to hurt mother. She had her reasons for not wanting me to know about my father. Really Michael, I'd rather not upset her."

Michael could hear the plea in Andrea's voice.

"Okay. We'll let the issue regarding your father pass, but you do have a right to know about your uncle."

Andrea smiled. "Yes. I want to know all about him and my aunt."

The two continued on, stopping in front of the newspaper building.

Michael got out and opened the door for Andrea. She stepped out of the car, purposely revealing her shapely legs to Michael. She stood up and put her arm around Michael's waist. The two walked into the building.

"Stop it," Michael whispered in her ear.

Andrea smiled, whispering, "You got me turned on. I want you."

Michael tried his best to ignore her.

Inside, the building was a beehive of activity. People running back and forth, newspaper print everywhere, strung across various desks. Phones ringing, people intent in their tasks. Andrea was in Michael's world. She was proud of him, the youngest editor of a major newspaper.

Andrea followed Michael through the maze of desks, noisy printing machines and ringing phones. Andrea was excited by the noise and apparent turmoil. Her world was organized, everything in order. She wanted to stop several times while traversing the building but Michael kept her for doing so.

The noise and excitement subsided floor by floor. Reaching the newspaper archives in the basement, the two were greeted by a short elderly woman with gray hair. A pair of glasses hung from around her neck.

"Good afternoon, Mr. Maxwell, Miss Maxwell. May I be of assistance to you?"

"Thank you, Lizzy," Michael replied. "I want to go through the old newspapers, twenty five to thirty years ago. I'm looking for the death of an Elizabeth Maxwell. The death would have been due to an automobile accident. Can you research the information on the computer?"

Lizzy hesitated.

"Lizzy, the information please. Now!" he commanded.

"Yes, Mr. Maxwell. Just give me a few minutes," she said nervously.

Lizzy walked over to the computer terminal and called up the research program. She input several bits of information. Responding to the computer's reply, she walked over to the CD file and withdrew several discs, placing one into the CD holder. The disc whirled, information flashed on the screen, then finalized with a message.

It states, DATA NOT PRESENT!

She continued with the process until finally, after several disc changes, the program stopped with single name.

"Elizabeth Gordon."

"Here you go, Mr. Maxwell. Is this what you're looking for?"

Michael walked to the monitor and read the reprint of the event as reported long ago.

"Mrs. Elizabeth Gordon of 13 Elm Street passed away. She was 76 years of age . . . "No!" Michael replied. "I'm looking for any information pertaining to an Elizabeth Maxwell."

Lizzy inputted additional information. Once again the computer terminal stopped at a single name.

"Elizabeth Maxwell." Press Enter For Data.

Lizzy gasped, "I thought I . . ."

She stopped short of completing what she was about to say. Michael glanced at her at the utterance. She reached to press the escape key when Michael suddenly grabbed her hand.

"Hold it!" Michael interrupted. "Key on that name please."

Lizzy reluctantly pressed the enter key. Within seconds, the data appeared on the monitor.

Michael read a recount of the obituary. Andrea stood next to him, reading along with him.

The report read, *"Miss Elizabeth Maxwell, age seventeen, succumbed from multiple injuries due to an auto accident. She is survived by . . ."* The report went on to list Andrea's grandparents and her mother. There was no mention of any other names.

Michael straightened up. "Lizzy, can you get me a date of this report?"

"Yes, sir," replied Lizzy. She input more request. The date January 12, 1966 flashed on the screen.

"Now search through all events up to three days prior to this report. Get me any information regarding Elizabeth Maxwell."

Lizzy entered information into the terminal. The disc whirled and clicked. A final message flashed on the screen. "Data Not Present."

Lizzy changed discs several times. Still the same message appeared.

Michael appeared puzzled. Lizzy, how far from the obit did you go?"

"A week, Mr. Maxwell."

Michael scratched his head. He looked at Andrea with a blank expression. Lizzy waited for further instructions.

"I'm looking for anything, anyone, perhaps a husband associated with Elizabeth Maxwell. Isn't there anything you can do to extract more information?"

"I can try something else," Lizzy said, while wringing her hands.

"Then do it!" Michael said impatiently.

Lizzy busied herself at the terminal, continuing to input information. All attempts to get additional information presented the same result.

Michael was perplexed. "Dead end. Where do we go from here?"

Lizzy did her best to avoid eye contact with Michael. He was about to give up, when Andrea tugged at his sleeve. He turned to her.

She whispered into his ear. "Darling I think she knows something but doesn't want us to find out."

Michael pondered the comment. "Okay Lizzy. I won't need you. You can go."

Lizzy did not move. "Mr. Maxwell, I have to get back to my work. I have a lot to do."

Michael looked at his watch. "That will be all Lizzy. You can go home now. Take the rest of the day off. I'll pay you for the full day."

Lizzy hesitated. She was about to reach over to turn off the terminal when Michael stopped her.

"Leave it on. I need to do some research."

Lizzy paused. "Do you know how to operate this terminal? Use the software?"

"I'll manage."

Lizzy got up from the chair, walked through the multitude of storage racks and left the room. Michael waited until he could hear the resounding slam of the basement door.

"Something's amiss here," he said, rubbing his chin.

"He sat down and began typing on the terminal keyboard. The computer processed the input date, finally stopping with message.

"Elizabeth Date Present. Three entries. Input additional information or press enter for all entries."

Michael looked up at Andrea. "Here we go."

He pressed the enter key. The computer presented the first bit of information regarding the person named Elizabeth.

"Elizabeth Everman, chairman of the garden club announces the monthly meeting . . ."

Michael hit the enter button. "Wrong Elizabeth."

Once again the computer disc whirled then stopped. The awaited information appeared on the screen.

"Miss Elizabeth Maxwell, daughter of Editor Mark Maxwell, died this evening from injuries sustained while riding in a Volkswagen. The driver (blank), believed to be her common-law husband, was found to be drunk. His impairment was the cause of the accident. No charges have been brought against the driver. The driver sustained severe injuries, however,

is expected to live. The couple had been living together for less than a year in a hippie commune. The parents refused comment, wishing to bury their child without fanfare."

Michael leaned back in the chair. "That's strange. Why couldn't Lizzy call up this information? And look at this! The driver's name, it's missing, and no charges against him."

Andrea looked at Michael, equally puzzled.

"We need the hard copy," he commented.

"Hard copy?" Andrea questioned.

"Yes, an actual print of the event."

Michael input more information into the computer. A date and hard copy location flashed on the screen.

"January 12, 1966, Rack A66, Compartment A."

Michael got up and motioned for Andrea to follow him.

The two walked among the dusty newspaper racks, stopping at the indicated rack and compartment. He counted down twelve newspapers and carefully withdrew the one dated January 12, 1966.

At the viewing table, he took the yellowed newspaper from its protective cover and began paging through it.

"Here it is," he said, after turning several pages.

The two read the account of the accident, just as it had appeared on the computer monitor. Without saying a word, they looked at each other.

Andrea expressed dismay.

"Michael! His name has been blotted out, with a marker. Why?"

"Someone went out their way to keep anyone from knowing the driver of the car," Michael commented.

He carefully paged through the aged newspaper, looking for more information. He turned to the society page, anticipating that there would be more information about the Maxwell family because of their notoriety. Just as expected, there was a small blurb written about Elizabeth and her death. Andrea read along with him, hopeful there might be a mention of her uncle's name. Any reference to the drivers name had been blotted out.

"Maybe we should leave it alone," Andrea said. "There's something sinister about all this, the name of the driver purposely being marked out. It's scary, gives me the creeps."

Michael looked at her. "No darling. There's much more than just a missing name. There's a story behind all of this. You ought to know by now, being in the newspaper business, stories are my bread and butter. Besides, I have an interest in anything concerning you."

Andrea was half listening to Michael. She haphazardly paged through the newspaper. She turned to the lead story on the front page.

"This is exciting," she said. "Just think, all this happened before you and I were born."

She read the headlines. *"Scientist Missing. Chemical scientist Andrew Simpson had been reported missing . . ."* The article continued on with details of the missing man.

"Hey!" exclaimed Andrea. "Look at this article. It's about an Andrew Simpson. That's the name of the new patient just admitted into the center, the man Mr. Fieldman had admitted. Do you think he's the same person?"

Michael read the article. "It's hard to say. I wouldn't expect someone being admitted to a rehabilitation center for an addiction is this man. The article indicates he was working on a secret government project. I imagine the government hid him away somewhere. Probably under an assumed name, for national security reason would be my best guess. Besides Simpson is a common name in this city."

Andrea looked up at Michael. "I suppose you're right. Where do we go from here? Maybe we should just drop the search."

Michael didn't reply. He folded the paper and put it back into the protective jacket, walked over to the rack and placed it back into its compartment.

Andrea stood at the viewing table, waiting for Michael to return. Michael stood for a few minutes, pondering the situation.

"Lizzy," he said quietly.

Michael walked back to where Andrea was standing. He glanced at his watch.

"Darling, I have to attend to something this afternoon. I'll drive you back to the center and catch up with you later this evening."

Andrea smiled. "But don't be late. I'd like to eat a little earlier this evening," she said, teasing.

Michael bent down and gave her a peck on the cheek.

"I'll meet you at the club. Five on the dot! Honest."

The two once again walked through the maze of newspaper storage racks, finally making their way to the entrance of the room Michael turned off the light and closed the door as they passed through it. Little was said as they walked to the car.

Michael appeared to be concentrating on something while driving back to the center. Andrea sat preoccupied with the scenery. He stopped in front of the center, got out and opened the door for Andrea.

"See you later," he said, then bent down and kissed her.

Andrea walked up to the doors, opened one and disappeared into the lobby. Assured she was safe, Michael got back into his car and drove off.

CHAPTER TEN

THE EVENTS AT the archives bothered Michael. As a reporter, he was trained to get the facts, no matter what the situation. He feared what the past might be hiding. The hidden events concerned his benefactor and Andreas' mother, as well as Andrea. He was apprehensive about what he might discover about the family.

He turned the car onto Broadmore Street, slowing to read the numbers on the houses. Coming to number 53, he stopped in front of a modest looking frame house. Switching off the engine, he sat for a few seconds to collect his thoughts. As he looked toward the front door, the curtain covering a front window parted for a few seconds, and then closed.

"She's home," Michael said to himself.

Michael stepped out of his car, walked up the pathway and onto the porch, stopping in front of the door. After adjusting his tie, he knocked on the front door.

Patiently he waited for someone to open the door. There was no response. He knocked again a little harder.

Several minutes passed. Suddenly he could hear the dead bolt latch clicking. The door knob turned and the door parted a few inches, limited by a safety chain.

"Yes?" Came an inquiry from an elderly woman's voice.

"Miss Arnold? It's me, Mr. Maxwell. May I come in?"

Lizzy hesitated, looking down at the porch floor.

"Yes, Mr. Maxwell," she said, while unlatching the chain and opening the door for him to enter.

Michael stepped into the foyer, closing the door behind him.

"Please, come into the parlor. We can talk there."

Michael followed Lizzy through the foyer, into the parlor. He took off his coat and set it on a sofa as he sat down. The room was adorned with furniture from the sixties, although showing little wear. There was an upright piano resting in one corner next to a fireplace. A small fire was burning.

"Would you like some coffee, Mr. Maxwell?"

"No thank you," Michael replied.

Lizzy sat on a chair opposite Michael. She glanced around nervously.

Michael was a flamboyant person, never bashful about what he wanted to say. Years of reporting toughened him, giving him the appearance of being insensitive toward events, situations and people that had information he needed. This meeting was different. Lizzy was a faithful employee, dedicated to her work. She had worked for the elder Mr. Maxwell, long before Michael was born. Michael did not want to upset her.

"Lizzy," he began, "I think you know why I'm here. It's about Elizabeth Maxwell, Mr. Maxwell's daughter and the circumstances surrounding her death. Information in the records is missing. Someone deleted and blotted out names on the hard copy as well as the computer. I surmise you were responsible for removing the information, since you alone maintain the old newspaper files and records. Did you remove the names?"

"Please, Mr. Maxwell," she said nervously. "I was just doing my job. Your father had me erase all references to Elizabeth's boyfriend. The Maxwell's are proud people, proper people. Mr. Maxwell didn't want anything or anybody to ruin their image, their name. I was just doing my job."

"Then you knew Elizabeth, her boyfriend? Everything?" he asked.

"Yes, I know everything," she said, turning away from Michael's glance. "I promised Mr. Maxwell I wouldn't say anything about him, Elizabeth's husband. It was a promise I made to Mar . . . , Mr. Maxwell."

Michael caught the slip. He stood up and walked around the parlor, thinking over the revelation. As he paced the room, he noticed a picture on top of the piano had been turned face down. We walked over and picked up the picture. Mark Maxwell was standing behind a beautiful, shapely brunette with his arm around her. She was wearing a scanty, revealing two piece bathing suit. The picture was taken at a beach.

Michael turned toward Lizzy. "Who is this with my father?" he asked. "What's this picture doing in your house?"

Lizzy lowered her head. "That was me, when I was younger."

Michael, looking at the photo, sized up the situation. His intuition gave him an insight as to what was going on at the time. He set the picture back down on the piano.

"Michael! Please," Lizzy begged. "I was young at the time. You can understand how I felt."

Michael turned toward Lizzy. "You never married. Why not? Judging by that photo, you were pretty enough, enough to have any man you wanted."

Lizzy turned away from Michael's stare. "I loved him."

"Loved whom? Mark? You almost mentioned him by his first name just a few minutes ago."

"Yes, I loved Mark. We were secret lovers. I cherished the few hours we spent together. I could never have enough of him. I would have done anything he asked. Anything."

"Were you working for the paper at the time?"

"Yes, in the archives. He used to come down often to see me. It was beautiful. We even made love down there. I loved him, Michael. I loved him."

Michael did not push any further. He knew what love could do to a person, how they could become irrational.

Lizzy was on the verge of tears. Michael walked over to her, setting down beside her. He took hold of her hand.

"Lizzy, what happened between you and Mr. Maxwell is history. I'll keep your secret. You need not fear anyone knowing what you've told me." He squeezed her hand gently.

Lizzy sighed. "Thank you, Mr. Maxwell."

"Now, what can you tell me about Elizabeth?"

Lizzy sighed. "She was somewhat wild," Lizzy replied. "Back then we all was caught up in the movement, free love and all that nonsense. I would like to think it was the best time of my life, but then I'm not so sure. Elizabeth and I were close friends, so I got to know the family. I'm sure she and her sister had an idea of what was going on between me and Mark. If Mrs. Maxwell knew about our affair, she didn't let on."

"What about her boyfriend? Elizabeth's boyfriend?"

"Her hippie boyfriend? Elizabeth started running around with him. He was a real character. Long hair, beads and all that stuff. Even Claire got caught up in the times and started doing the same, thinking it was the in thing to do, wanting to be with the in crowd. Eventually Claire came back to reality. She married and settled down. Her husband worked for a company contracted by the government. I never knew what he did at the company. He'd just say it was a secret government project and wasn't allowed talking about it to anyone outside of the company."

"Claire married a hippie?" Michael said with a smile.

"Yes, sort of, but the marriage didn't work. He left Claire not long after they were married. She was carrying Andrea at the time but he never knew about the child."

"Left? You mean he was killed in Vietnam."

"Uh . . . Yes! I believe he was killed in Vietnam." Lizzy affirmed, haphazardly, turning her glance away from Michael.

"So what happened to Elizabeth and her boyfriend?"

Lizzy sighed again. "It was a mess. She was only a year younger than Claire. As I said, she was wild, always running around with her hippie boyfriend. She became a real flower child. She opposed everyone, her sister, and her parents. She rebelled against everyone. Finally she left home and lived with him, in one of the communes. It bothered me deeply. Mark tried to have me intervene, to bring her back. All my efforts, as well as Claire's, failed. It really upset Mark."

"How did she react, knowing she was having a negative effect on her father?"

"She didn't care. It was though she had become a different person. She began to appear in rallies, carrying banners, opposing everything, everyone, the newspaper, doing whatever she pleased to aggravate the establishment."

"And her boyfriend?"

"He was right along side her. He was her inspiration. It really hurt me to see her doing this to herself. I tried to tell her it was a temporary movement. It would lead her nowhere."

"But she wouldn't listen," Michael intoned.

"Unfortunate as it was, she wouldn't listen. Then one day, the two of them were riding in their Volkswagen. He was drunk or high on marijuana or something. Rounding a curve, he missed and the car went over a cliff. She was killed instantly, being thrown out of the windshield. He was banged up, but managed to live. He required extensive surgery, which left him disfigured and partially lame."

"Were they common-law married?" Michael asked.

Lizzy paused. "Well . . . yes, to start with they were."

"What do you mean to start?" Michael questioned.

"They were married. Legally, that is," Lizzy replied. "At first they lived together, never giving marriage a thought. Later both of them came to me and told me they wanted to get married. Make it legal. Elizabeth said it was her way of opposing her father, what he stood for and the love she professed for her boyfriend."

"Why is it no one knows of their marriage?"

"It was a secret. The two went across the state line and got married by a justice of the peace. I was there. I witnessed the marriage, along with a friend of mine. In this state seventeen was too young to marry without your parents' permission. In our neighboring state, sixteen was a legal marrying age without parental consent. The two got fake documents that showed they lived in the state so no question would be asked."

"Who else witnessed the marriage?"

Lizzy evaded the question, looking across the room.

"Just someone in the commune," she said finally. "I can't recall his name."

Michael let her answer pass. "Was it the times or did they really love one another?"

"They were definitely in love. It wasn't just infatuation. It broke his heart when Elizabeth died. It was as though he had lost the will to live."

"It's obvious you knew Elizabeth's boyfriend, or should say husband well."

"Yes, I knew him."

"What was he like?"

"Smart even brilliant. He had the ability to see through all the false fronts that people put on. I think this is one reason why a lot of people didn't care for him. He could put you down with ease. It was a natural trait he had. I was envious of his ability, even secretly loved him but kept my distance for Elizabeth's sake. She was like a sister to me."

Michael tried to hide his astonishment. "If Mr. Maxwell was so set on keeping negative events concerning his family out of public view, how did the report managed to get into the paper when his daughter was killed?"

"That was really something. Mark was furious when the article was printed in his paper. He was so mad; he fired the reporter who wrote the article and the society page editor for allowing it to be published. Mark was away at the time the article appeared. He eventually had a meeting with all his staff members, telling them his family was off-limits and, except with his permission, nothing was to be printed about the family."

"Is that when he had you remove the name of Elizabeth's husband?"

"Yes. He came to me in the library and told me to erase any printed reference to her boyfriend. Later, when we updated the files and got computers, he had me to do the same when I put the data into the computers hard drive and storage discs."

"How long did you continue seeing Mark?"

"The relationship began to wane shortly after Elizabeth's death. He became a different man, preoccupied with his remaining daughter Claire, and the birth of his granddaughter. He kept away from me, although I admit, I still loved him."

"Why did he still let you work at the paper?"

Lizzy looked away. I don't know. He did take care of me, making sure I got my raises and periodic bonuses. I truly think there was still something there between us. I'm sure he was being extra cautious, afraid our affair would be found out and his name splattered across other newspapers."

"So you kept quiet all these years?"

"Yes. In time, news about his daughter died down. The years passed and people forgot. When you came along, he adopted you out of the orphanage. His whole life changed once again. I watched from afar as he took you under his wing. I was happy for you."

"You moved into the background."

"Yes." Lizzy paused with a solemn look on her face. "I suppose it was proper. With Elizabeth's death and you, I was pushed back, forgotten. Even Claire evaded me. I still feel linked to the family even after all these years."

"Do you have any regrets?"

"What is there to regret? I control my life. Why should I have any regrets?" she said, sternly. "Sure my life didn't turn out like I had hoped. But then, I'm not alone. There are thousand of others like myself whose lives haven't turned out like they had wished."

Michael blushed realizing he had touched a nerve in Lizzy unintentionally.

He paused to let Lizzy get over his visit and the wealth of information she had revealed. She was quietly watching Michael.

"It's not ended. Is it Mr. Maxwell?" she asked.

Michael looked at her in surprise. "What do you mean?"

"You know what I mean. You want his name. You want to know the name of Elizabeth's husband."

He smiled. "Yes! For Andrea's sake."

She got up from the chair and walked over to Michael. She sat down beside him.

"I'll tell you what you ask, but let me warn you. You'll open up a deep secret about the family. Are you sure you want to know?"

Andrea has a right to know about her uncle. He's still family, regardless of what happened."

"Well then, what I'm about to tell you, you must use with utmost caution. The information can change the lives of all concerned."

Michael looked at Lizzy with a puzzled expression. "I'll be careful."

"As you wish," she said. "His name is now Marty Fieldman.

CHAPTER ELEVEN

MICHAEL GLANCED AT her. "That name sounds familiar. There was a Marty Fieldman at the rehabilitation center earlier this morning. Could he be the same person?"

"I don't know. It's possible. What does he look like? His facial features? Does he walk with a limp?"

Michael recalled the chance meeting with Marty. "As I recall, his face was somewhat scarred and had half an ear missing. Andrea pointed that out and he did walk with a slight limp."

"Andrea was there when you met him?"

"Of course. Is he the Marty Fieldman you're talking about?"

"Yes. He's Andrea's uncle Martin."

"Martin?" he questioned. "Don't you mean Marty?"

"It was Martin a long time ago. Martin Phelpman. He changed his name to Marty Fieldman."

"Why the name change?"

"I'm not sure. My guess is it was the only way he could keep his privacy."

"If he's the same person you knew so long ago, then Claire surely knows about him."

"She knows all about Marty."

"Why all of a sudden, after all these years, is he making an appearance?"

"I don't know." Lizzy said. "What was he doing at the center? Was he there to see Claire?"

"Andrea mentioned, he was supposed to be sponsoring a patient, someone by the name Andrew Simpson."

Lizzy turned around abruptly, about to say something but checked herself.

"You were about to say?" Michael questioned.

Lizzy stood up and walked to the parlor window. Several moments passed before she said anything further.

"Please, I beg you. Leave it alone. Marty Fieldman mustn't come back into their lives. It can be damaging to you and Andrea."

Michael was taken back by the sudden plea. "Why? What could he do? How would Andrea knowing about her uncle be damaging to her or any of us for that matter?"

"It's more than just her knowing her uncle. It goes much deeper. There are secrets, more than you could ever imagine. Things that affect you Andrea, Claire and me. Please, let the past be."

Lizzy had piqued his curiosity. He wanted to know what was hidden in her mind, her past.

"If what you know is so terrible, why not tell me and get it out of your system. It's obvious this thing this hidden past of yours is tormenting you and has for a long time. What is it?"

Lizzy was on the verge of tears. Despite her attempts to hold back the tears, they began to stream down her face.

"Oh Michael," she said, "It's you! It's you and Andrea I don't want to harm."

Michael got up and walked over to Lizzy. He felt compassion for her, sensing she had gone through a lot over the years, being taken advantage of and having to play second fiddle to the Maxwell family. He took a hold of her and put his arms around her in an attempt to comfort her. She buried her head in his chest, as she continued crying without letting up.

Michael said little. He held her, waiting for her to get the pain out of her system. The two stood for several minutes. The tears began to subside, trailing off to an occasional sob. She got up and walked over to a credenza, pulled out several tissues from the tissue box on it and blotted away the tears.

Apprehensive, Michael asked, "How could you hurt me or Andrea? Why would you want to? I'm nothing to you except your employer."

"Believe me, Michael; I don't want to hurt you in any way. It's what you don't know."

"What I don't know?"

"Yes," Lizzy replied. "It's what you don't know about the situation that can be damaging. It's about you. How you come to be in the orphanage. Why Mr. Maxwell adopted you and gave you his name."

A strange feeling came over Michael. He had always wondered what had happened to him as an infant. What the circumstance was that caused him to be placed in the orphanage. The only information he could find out about was he had been put in a basket and placed near the front door of the orphanage. Attached to the clothes he was wearing was pinned a note with the single word, "Michael" Not knowing his last name, the authorities at the orphanage had given him a last name of Tuesday. Michael Tuesday, because it was the day of the week he was found on the front steps.

At the age of two, Mr. Maxwell, although advanced in years, had adopted Michael and raised him as his son, giving him the Maxwell name. Michael enjoyed the pleasures and benefits of being raised a Maxwell.

A smile came to Michael's face as he thought of the strange situation surrounding him and Andrea. Through adoption, Michael was in reality Andrea's uncle. The two, each being of the same age, had grown up together. They went to the same private schools and college together. Now they were to be married. He wondered what the tabloids would have to say about the strange relationship.

Claire had considered Michael a younger brother although she could never bring herself to become close to him. She was disturbed when Andrea had fallen in love with him and on being told the two intended to marry. She did her best not to encourage the relationship between them and was intent on preventing the two marrying. Andrea knew what her mother was attempting to do but ignored her subtle dislike for what was happening.

Life was going the way Michael wanted. He was editor of the newspaper, even though it was owned by Claire, being passed to her when Mr. Maxwell had passed away. Mr. Maxwell had groomed Michael for the position, wanting him to be the editor when his time came to give up the reins.

The position of editor was not simply given to him. Michael had worked hard, learning every aspect of the newspaper business from copy boy, reporter, all the way up to editor. It was a natural chain of events. It was his destiny.

At the insistence of her father and not wanting to be bogged down with the business end of the newspaper, Claire made Michael the editor, giving him complete control over it.

Claire was dedicated to being a doctor even though she did not have to work. She enjoyed helping others, often donating her time to help those in need. She devoted her time to helping those afflicted with drugs and alcoholism.

Michael walked over to Lizzy. "Now tell me," he said, "what's so terrible about the past?"

Lizzy walked back to the sofa and sat down. She could not bring herself to look at Michael.

"I'm not going to leave until you tell me what's bothering you Lizzy. What are you hiding?"

"Please, Michael," she pleaded. "You needn't know. Your life is perfect. You're successful. You have the world at your feet. Why let me ruin it?"

Michael forced a laugh. "I really don't think anything you have to say can ruin my life"

"I'm not so sure."

"That is the second time you made that comment. Now tell me, what you don't want me to know?" Michael demanded.

Lizzy repositioned herself on the couch. "Alright, I'll tell you, but please forgive me. I love you too much and couldn't bear to see you hurt."

"You love me?" questioned Michael.

Lizzy looked up at him. "I've always loved you. From the day you were born, throughout your life. You became part of the Maxwell family, so there was no way I was able to get near you. I had to love you from a distance."

Michael was surprised at her admiration for him. He assumed because of his looks, it was an infatuation an older woman had for him. He was her employer. He had often noticed Lizzy looking at him whenever he had an occasion to come down to do some research in the archives.

Michael sat down next to Lizzy. He took hold of her hand.

"What can be so terrible?"

Lizzy looked away. "I know who put you in the basket and placed you on the orphanage steps."

"What do you mean you know? Who? Tell me."

Lizzy began to sob again. "I put you there. I put you on the orphanage steps."

"You!" he exclaimed.

"Yes. It was me."

Michael was stunned. "You? Why would you put me there?"

"It was because of the circumstances. You can't marry Andrea. You just can't."

"Why shouldn't I marry Andrea?"

"She's your half niece."

"What do you mean my half niece? How can that be? I'm an orphan. You said you placed me at the orphanage."

Lizzy cleared her throat. "I'll tell you how you came to be placed in the orphanage. Why I placed you there. You see, I was involved with Mr. Maxwell. We had an affair as I have told you. What you don't know is . . ." Lizzy couldn't bring herself to continue.

"What don't I know?" Michael asked impatiently.

Lizzy swallowed hard. "What you don't know is I got pregnant by Mr. Maxwell. When I told him, he denied it was his child. After convincing him the baby was his, he begged me to have an abortion, offering to take me to a distant state to have one. He tried to bribe me. I just couldn't go through with it. I didn't want to have an abortion and ignored his plea. I knew this would be the end of the relationship but I loved him. Having his child, I thought, was my only hold at being close to him."

"A concocted story, a fabrication!" Michael shouted. "A story to hold him in your clutches."

"No Michael," she said. "Things began to go wrong with the family. Elizabeth leaving home to live in the commune, her death, Claire's husband leaving her. A lot happened in a very short time. Mark was caught up with the events of the times. He forgot about me."

"So what did you do?"

"What could I do? I had the child, to Marks dismay. I took a leave of absence from work, making an excuse that I had a sick relative to look after. I was gone from the paper the entire term of my pregnancy. Of course, very few people knew I was pregnant. I stayed out of circulation, living with a cousin. I had the baby, a beautiful little boy."

Michael sensed what she was about to say, surmising it wasn't going to be good news.

"Who was the boy?"

"It was you," she said. "You're my son. Mr. Maxwell is your father, your real father."

Michael shook his head. "It can't be. You can't be my mother. Tell me so."

"I wish I could. But it's the truth. You are my son."

"So," he said, barely able to form the words as he choked, "if you are my mother, why did you abandon me?"

"What could I do?" Lizzy said. "I was a single girl and pregnant. Only a few people knew I was seeing Mr. Maxwell secretly. How was I to explain getting pregnant by him? Theirs was a proper family, an outstanding family in the community. Who would have believed I was having his child? People would have suspected I made up the story. I couldn't let that happen to me, Mr. Maxwell. Besides, I had my own life to live."

"So you dumped me on the orphanage steps?"

"No. I didn't just dump you. You were my child. I loved you. I nurtured you for almost a year, hiding you from those who knew me. In time the little money I had saved dwindled. I had to return to work, my home. Mark longed for a son to follow in his footsteps. So he started scheming and began to use me, even threatened me, saying he'd report me to the child protection agency claiming I was abusing you and was a drug addict."

"Some mother," he said contemptuously.

Lizzy began to cry again. She did not hold back the flow tears streaming down her face. Michael held fast. He refused to believe her.

"Then I contend, it's a fabrication," he said. "An attempt to hold on to the Maxwell family. Why else would you concoct such a story? To get what you feel is rightfully yours because of the affair you had with Mark Maxwell."

Lizzy snapped, "No! I don't care about the Maxwell fortune. All I care about is you and what happens to you. You can't marry Andrea. She's your niece."

"What proofs have you that you're my mother, besides a piece of paper? Birth certificates can be faked."

Lizzy straightened up. "There is one other who knows about me and Mr. Maxwell."

Michael was getting tired of the game. "Who, who is the mysterious person that might know about you, Mr. Maxwell and me?"

Lizzy looked at Michael. "Marty Fieldman, he knew Elizabeth and I were close friends. She knew as well as Marty, I was pregnant."

Michael thought over what Lizzy had revealed. Still skeptical, he asked, "Where was I born?"

Lizzy hesitated. "Hadden Hospital."

"What state" he demanded.

Lizzy did not respond.

Michael picked up his coat and put it on. He looked down at Lizzy. "I refuse to believe you," he said.

Lizzy looked up. "Michael, I love you. I didn't want to tell you these things. Believe me all I've told you is true."

Michael turned and walked toward the front door. He opened it, stepped outside and walked to his car. Unlocking the door, he got in and put the key into the ignition, starting the engine. He glanced back toward the house. Lizzy stood in the doorway. She still was crying. Michael drove off.

As he headed for the rehabilitation center, he was confused and hurt. He could not bring himself to believe what Lizzy had told him. Although he had his doubts, he was antagonized by what Lizzy had revealed to him.

Maneuvering his car through the city streets, he finally stopped in front of the center and walked toward the main entrance. Opening the door, he passed through the lobby and walked directly to Claire's office. On reaching her office, he opened the door and stepped inside.

Claire looked up as the door opened. "Michael, what a surprise," she said coolly."

Michael walked to her desk and sat in the chair beside it.

"Claire," he said. "Who's Marty Fieldman, better known as Martin Phelpman?"

"Martin Phelpman? Marty Fieldman? I don't understand. Why the questioning?" she replied defensively.

Michael glared at her. "You know, Claire. You know about this man. Who is he?"

Claire evaded his eyes. "If you insist, he's just someone I knew in the past. He's of no concern to you."

"Of no concern!" Michael blurted. "He is Andreas' uncle. That's my concern! Lizzy told me he was Elizabeth's husband."

Claire squirmed in her chair. "You spoke to Lizzy?"

"Yes. And you knew her and ran around with her in the past. Am I correct?"

Claire's face reddened. "Only for a short period. We were all close back then but when I got married I quit running around with that crowd and ended any association with her."

"Just like that? What was the real reason for your dissociation between you two?"

"She was a nobody. A nothing! Just someone we knew. Lizzy was a harlot. She would have sex with any man crossing her path. Sure she messed around with my father a few times. He was having a mid-life crisis thing. Dad had a few flings with her, but that was short lived."

"She claims your father got her pregnant!"

Claire glanced at him. "Do you really believe that? She could have been impregnated by any of the men she slept with."

"She had a pretty convincing argument," Michael replied, "although I have difficulty believing her. She has a picture of her and your father together. The picture seemed fairly compromising to me and makes me wonder if it was just a fling. It doesn't take a mystic to see what was happening."

"Dad was foolish at the time, Michael. Lizzy was just some passing fancy, a sex object for him."

"She seems to know you and Elizabeth pretty well, and don't deny associating with her."

"No. She was my father's love interest at the time. I didn't think anything of it back then. It was a time of free love. Anything goes. Free love was in. You weren't there. You wouldn't understand."

"Did your mother know what was going on?"

"She didn't know. Besides, Mother held onto her Victorian virtues. You know that from being raised by her. We didn't see anything wrong with dad having an affair. From what we could see, he probably wasn't having sex with mother anyway."

"You called it free love. Adultery is more like it," Michael retorted.

"You don't understand what the times were like," Claire retorted in defense. "It was the start of a new era, an era of self-expression, love, to care truly for one another. We were open, uninhibited."

"Lizzy? What about her? You claim love but you abandoned her. Why?"

"Being a Maxwell, I had an image to uphold, and Lizzy certainly was not part of that image."

"What about this Martin Phelpman? How does he fit in this picture? You can't deny knowing him."

Claire repositioned herself in her chair. "Yes, I know about Martin."

"Is he your brother-in-law, Andrea's uncle?"

Claire paused.

"Answer me!" Michael demanded.

"Yes. Martin is my brother-in-law. He was married to my sister Elizabeth. Are you satisfied now?"

"How do you know this?"

"Lizzy was at the wedding. She was a witness. Elizabeth ran around with all of them, lived in the commune. She began to worry and decided she had better get married. Legally that is."

"You loved Elizabeth? What about Martin?"

"Yes I loved Elizabeth. She was my sister. How could I not love her? Martin? I don't know. I suppose I did love him in a sense, but then he killed her."

"He killed her?" Michael said, surprised at her answer. "He may have been responsible for her death but he didn't kill her."

"Same thing," Claire replied.

"So you and the family cut him out of your lives, just as a doctor cuts a cancer out of a patient. How can you be so cruel, so insensitive? He's still family regardless of what happened."

"Not a member of our family." Claire snapped.

"I don't believe you"

Claire didn't reply. She peered at Michael, pausing to collect her thoughts.

"Don't you think he's suffered enough? I had a chance meeting with Mr. Fieldman earlier this morning in the lobby. I got a good look at him. He's disfigured, lame. He still carries the scars of the accident. I'm sure he's grieved the loss of Elizabeth. Don't you think it's high time you have a little compassion? Forgave the man?"

Claire turned away from Michael. She sighed. "What's the use? I don't hate Martin. Never did. I just didn't want him getting close to Andrea. I told him never to come near her."

"Why?"

"Because of what he knows," she replied quietly.

"What does that mean? What does he know?"

"He knows her father."

"Knew," Michael interjected. "Maybe he knew her father. He's dead. Remember, killed in Vietnam."

Claire turned toward Michael. Tears were streaming down her face. "He wasn't killed in Vietnam. He's still alive."

"What? Still alive? Wasn't killed in Vietnam? You know about Andrea's father still being alive and didn't tell her?"

"Michael," she sobbed, "He left me, just disappeared. He never bothered to contact me. He doesn't even know he has a daughter."

Michael stood up. "Wait a minute. I've got to clear my head."

He paced the floor, occasionally glancing at Claire. She had stopped crying. She could not bring herself to look at him.

He suddenly stopped pacing, glancing at Claire.

"There's more to this story and I feel you're hiding something. I want to know who Andrea's father is."

"Please, Michael," she pleaded, "Don't make me tell you. Andrea mustn't know. She can't know."

"I'll find out from Lizzy."

The tears began to flow once again. "Alright, he's Andrew, Andrew Simpson. He's the patient Marty admitted earlier this week.

Michael was floored. "You mean Andrea has her father as a patient and doesn't even know?"

Claire nodded.

Michael walked over to the couch and sat down. He was bewildered. For once in his life, he was at a total loss for words, realizing what this information would do to Andrea.

"So, the cat's out of the bag. What could be worse?" he said.

Claire got up from the chair and walked toward the window. She gazed outside. "There's more," she said.

Michael looked up at her. "Well, this seems to be the day of confessions. I feel like a damned priest. What other information do you have? My day is already ruined. What could be worse?"

"It concerns you," she said.

"What about me?"

"It concerns Lizzy Arnold and you."

Michael was apprehensive, fearing what she would say. "Go on. Tell me."

"Lizzy Arnold is your mother, just as she told you. You would have found out eventually, so I may as well be truthful, and Mark Maxwell is your real father."

Michael put his hand to his face. "Oh my God!" he exclaimed.

The two remained silent. Claire continued looking out the window.

Michael took a handkerchief from his pocket and dried a tear that managed to well up in his eyes. He could still smell Andrea's perfume on it from earlier in the day.

Claire turned around and walked toward the couch. She sat down next to him.

"Michael, please forgive me. I didn't want this to happen. I tried my best to protect you and Andrea. You two have a full life together ahead of you. I know you love Andrea and she loves you. Let this thing pass. Put it behind you. You and Andrea can be close as family. Don't let it bother you."

Michael pulled away. "How can you be so unsympathetic? What about Andrea? That means I'm her half uncle. What about her father? How are you going to explain him to Andrea, and Marty Fieldman being her uncle by marriage? What about him? You're cold, Claire. How can you be so cold?"

Claire looked away. "Don't be so hard on me. This situation would have eventually have had to happen. It's best it did before you and Andrea married."

"And Lizzy?" he said, cutting her short. "What about my mother? What kind of pain has she been going through all these years, watching me growing up in the Maxwell mansion, having to love me from a distance. What about her Claire?"

Claire remained silent fearing she might reveal what she did not want Michael to know under the circumstances. She could not bring herself to look at him again.

Michael suddenly stood up. "I've got to go. I have to get out of here, go somewhere to collect my thoughts."

He walked toward the door, opened it and stepped out. Having second thoughts, Claire ran after him.

"Michael!" she called.

Michael didn't bother to look back. He walked down the corridor, through the lobby and out the main entrance. Reaching his car, he unlocked the door, opened it and sat down.

Several minutes having passed he put the key in the ignition, starting the car and headed down the winding driveway out of the rehabilitation center complex.

Michael drove to the private club he frequented. The bartender on duty noticed Michael as he entered.

"Good afternoon, Mr. Maxwell," the bartender greeted. "You're early today."

Michael looked at him. "Good afternoon, Josh. Give me my usual, and make it a double."

The bartender pondered Michael a moment. Dutifully he set about pouring the double scotch as requested and handed it to him.

"Thanks," Michael said. "Put it on my tab."

Michael took the drink and headed for a booth. Sitting down, he began to sip the scotch. The events of the day clouded his mind. Never in his life had he been so confused, lost at what to do.

Michael finished his drink. He motioned for the bartender to make him another.

Once again the bartender did as commanded, taking it to where Michael was sitting. He set the drink down on the table and waited.

"You can leave," he said, without looking up. "It's my problem."

"Michael! Mr. Maxwell, you can't bury your problems in drink. It doesn't work."

Michael squeezed the glass as hard as he could. The glass relented, breaking in his hand. Tears fell from his eyes as the blood oozed from his hand.

Josh withdrew a clean bar towel from around his waist and carefully wrapped Michael's hand.

"This is beyond you, Mr. Maxwell."

Michael looked up at him "What am I to do?"

Josh tended to his hand. "You have to face the problem. Nothing in life is worth drowning your problems in drink. Go ahead. Get out of here, Mr. Maxwell."

Michael stood up and looked at his hand.

"It'll be fine. Just a slight cut. Nothing serious," Josh said.

Michael turned and walked into the men's room, stopping in front of a sink. He put his hand under the faucet after turning it on, rinsing the blood from his hand. He dried his hands on a paper towel then walked out.

Josh watched as Michael opened the door and departed the club.

Michael walked back to his car, got in and drove to Broadmore Street. Once again he stopped in front of Lizzy's house.

He sat in the car, pondering the situation. He knew what he had to do. He walked up the path, onto the porch. He paused, and then knocked.

"Yes," the familiar voice questioned.

"Lizzy, it's Michael." he replied softly.

Lizzy opened the door to let him in. She did not look at him when he stepped into the foyer.

"What is it? What do you want now?" Lizzy asked.

Michael paused as he closed the door behind him. He took Lizzy in his arms. She looked up at him, startled by his action.

He said a single word. "Mother!"

"Oh Michael, you know! You believe me," she cried, while burying her head in his chest.

CHAPTER TWELVE

ANDREW WAS SITTING in a chair set next to the window in his room. He was reading the newspaper which was delivered to each patient's room while they ate breakfast. This was his third week in the rehabilitation center. The several medications given him daily when he first entered to help him overcome his addiction and to prevent the onslaught of the DT's had been slowly reduced to two Methadone tablets a day. This was the week the program called for weaning him off all medications used to combat his addiction completely.

Andrea tapped lightly on the door, and then entered his room.

Andrew was expecting one of the nurses who delivered his daily medication each morning to be entering the room. He was surprised when Andrea entered the room instead.

"Good morning Mr. Simpson, how are you feeling this morning?" she asked.

Andrew rested the newspaper he was reading on his lap and looked up at her. "I feel fine doctor, except for the occasional back pain, I feel fine."

She glanced at the newspaper. "It's very satisfying to see you taking interest in what's happening in our city. Do you read the paper every day?"

"Yes. I do now," he replied.

"How's that desire for alcohol doing? Do you still have a craving for it?"

"No, not like I did before I came here. In fact it hasn't even entered my mind for the past several days."

"Wonderful. It's looks as though we are making good progress with our program."

She glanced at his chart and made some notation on it. "Now comes the real test," she said.

"Real test?" he asked.

"Yes. This is the week we will try weaning you off all the medications we use to help you battle your addiction. Except for the medication ordered by your oncologist, the others we use for you addiction will slowly be eliminated. By mid week you should be completely off them."

"Is that a good thing? Getting off all that medication you're talking about?"

"Hopefully it will be, although it might get a little rough for you without them. We'll see. If necessary, we'll put you back on them if the need arises."

"Good. I hope I don't need them then. I'm about ready to get out of here. I really want to get back to work."

"So you feel as though you've made enough progress you can leave our center?"

Andrew smiled. "I believe so. I think I've made it, really kicked my alcohol addiction."

"Good. By the end of the week, perhaps you'll be able to leave our center. We'll see. Do . . ."

"You're so beautiful," he suddenly commented, stopping her from what she was about to ask him. "You remind me of someone I once knew."

"Now Mr. Simpson, you've got to get over this fascination you appear to have toward me even though I remind you of a past acquaintance. Now do you think you can leave here without any hang-ups? Be able to meet the public without any fears?"

"Yes. I believe I can," he replied, although appearing to be preoccupied with other thoughts as he continuously gazed at her.

Andrea was aware of Andrew's eyes following her every move. She had never experienced a patient so intense while they communicated. The intense ogling and resulting comments from him annoyed her. She felt she had better resolve this issue before allowing him to leave the center.

"You must get over this infatuation you have for me. Every time we meet you always do and say these same things."

"You do remind me of someone. Of someone I knew in the past," he quickly intoned.

Andrea watched Andrew for a few moments, contemplating his admiration for her. She wondered what was hidden so deep in his mind. Previous sessions did not reveal any inner problems or the root cause of this dilemma. She decided she had better force it out into the open.

"Andrew," she said. "I'd like to put you back under hypnosis. Something in your past may be affecting your present real world thinking and I'd like to see if there's anything bothering you subconsciously. This constant fascination you have for me is appearing to be a problem lurking in your subconscious mind and we need to get it out in the open so we can address the issue. Do you understand?"

"Sure. If it'll help," he commented.

"Wonderful. Please lay down on the bed."

Andrew got up, carefully folded the newspaper, put it on the night stand then got onto the bed as she requested.

Andrea sat on the side of the bed.

"You've been through this hypnosis procedure in earlier sessions, so it'll be much easier for you to experience a trance. I'll count backward from ten. You'll fall asleep before I reach one. You'll respond to my voice and reply to any questions I ask. You'll hear nothing but my voice. Ready."

Andrew looked up at her and nodded.

"Here we go. Ten, nine, eight . . ."

Andrew fell into a deep trance.

"Andrew, when I count to three you'll awaken and answer my questions as best you can. Do you understand?"

"Yes," he replied in a monotone voice.

She counted to three and Andrew opened his eyes.

"Who does Doctor Andrea Maxwell remind you of?" she asked.

Andrew stirred, appearing uncomfortable.

"Her. Long time ago. Her," he said after a short delay.

"Who?" she questioned. "What was the person's name?"

"Claire," he responded.

"Does she have a last name, this Claire?"

Andrew hesitated.

"Andrew, what was her last name?"

"Simpson," he answered.

"Why is this Claire locked in your mind? What was she to you?"

Again he hesitated before answering. Andrea waited. After a slight delay he answered, "She was my wife."

"What happened to her?"

"She's gone. I'm gone. Left. Died."

The answers did not make sense to Andrea. "You're gone, or is she gone?" Andrea questioned.

"Yes. Gone. Died. Government ruined me. I'm dead. Nothing."

The reply puzzled Andrea. She now realized in his subconscious a problem existed he continued to fight. She knew she had to bring his subconscious to the forefront and have him face it. She decided to bring him out of his hypnotic state to address the issue.

"Andrew, I'm going to count to three. You'll come out of your sleep and feel refreshed when I reach the count of three. One, two, three."

Andrew looked up at Andrea.

"How do you feel?" she asked.

"Okay. Did you find out what you wanted to know?"

"Only partly. Who is Claire?"

Andrew turned away.

"Andrew, who is she?"

"She was someone I knew a long time ago," he answered quietly.

"Did you love her?"

"Yes, I loved her very much."

"What happened to her?"

"She pushed too hard. I was working for the government back then, developing a secret chemical. The government decided to use my development for the Vietnam War. I didn't want to do it but she kept pushing. That terrible chemical. I made it. I developed it."

"What terrible chemical did you develop?"

"It was a defoliant called Agent something, I not sure of the full name."

"Oh come now, Andrew what's so terrible about developing a defoliant."

"It caused cancer and was very deadly. Do you hear me? It was very deadly," he replied, raising his voice.

Seeing he was becoming distraught, Andrea weighed her words, being careful not to cause any further anxiety.

"There's no conclusive evidence the chemical agent you speak of causes cancer," she said. "It's only suspected and has yet to be proven."

"It does," he rebutted.

Andrea looked at him in amazement. "Where did you work when you and this Claire were together?"

"At the laboratory. BMD Corporation."

"What was your position with the company?"

"I was a chemist."

"What did you do when you suspected your development was harmful to humans?"

"Nothing!"

"Nothing? You just let the government go ahead and use it in Vietnam, convinced it was a dangerous chemical?"

"The government decided to use the agent in Vietnam, despite my findings. I didn't protest. I did nothing."

"You did nothing?"

"I couldn't handle it. They wouldn't listen to me. I felt terrible knowing what would happen if they used it. I even called the General responsible for the decision to use the chemical, telling him of my findings. I pleaded with him. He wouldn't listen. It was then I decided to disappear. I didn't want to have anything further to do with the chemical knowing thousands of our soldiers, civilians and anybody inhaling the dust particles would be afflicted."

"Disappear?" she said, as she stood up.

"Andrew glanced up at her. "As I said, I couldn't handle it. The pressure from the plant, Claire, and knowing what would happen to anyone coming in contact with concentrated doses of the chemical."

Andrea paced the room. She recalled the newspaper article about a missing scientist. She turned around abruptly.

"When did this take place? When did you leave the plant, quit your job and decide to disappear?"

He turned his head in her direction. "In the sixties."

"You're the one that was reported missing in the papers. Weren't you?"

He looked at her with a surprise expression, and then smiled. "Yes," he replied.

"Where did you go? Where did you hide?"

"Oh it was easy. Lots of hippie communes back then. I dropped out of society, became a hippie. I went on the road, traveling from city to city."

"What about Claire? Your wife? Did you not have any feelings for her?"

"Yes, I cared for her," he replied with a slight quiver in his voice. "I loved her and still do but I couldn't take her pushing."

"What happened to her?"

"I don't know. I guess she divorced me after I left. I don't really know."

"Yet you came back here. Surely you tried to locate her."

"By then it was too late. I took to the bottle, lost all pride. All I cared about was getting enough to drink, living day by day. I didn't care about anything or the world around me."

"What drew you back to this city?" Andrea questioned. "You could have remained anywhere but you chose to come back. Why?"

Andrew turned his back toward Andrea, not wanting to face her. "Because of Claire," he said.

"Tell me something about your Claire."

"Rich. Very important family," he replied, while rolling over and staring at the ceiling. "She was a member of a very prominent family."

Andrea paused with her questioning. She glanced down at Andrew, wondering. Her heart began to beat rapidly. A tingling sensation came over her. She felt Andrew was a connection to her past but was not sure.

In anticipation she asked again, "What was the name of your wife?"

"Claire. Claire Simpson. I told you that before."

"What was her name before you married her?" she asked.

"Claire Maxwell."

Andrea was stunned, barely able to continue with her questioning. Trying to control the emotions beginning to well up insider her, she asked, "Did the two of you have any children?"

Andrew turned away from her glance. "No," he replied.

Andrea felt relieved, although perplexed, discovering her mother was married more than once before she was born.

The lull in the questioning bothered Andrew. "Is something wrong?"

"Did your wife have any sisters or brothers?"

"Yes. She had a sister, no brothers."

Andrea felt she was on the verge of finding out who her uncle was. In anticipation, she asked, "What was her name? What was the name of her sister?"

"Elizabeth."

"Was it Elizabeth Maxwell?" she questioned in anticipation.

Andrew glanced at her with a blank expression on his face. "Of course it was Elizabeth Maxwell," he answered. "The two were sisters."

"Did Elizabeth have a boyfriend?"

Andrew paused, looking puzzled. "I don't know what my past and the people I ran around with have to do with my recovery," he said.

"It's important," Andrea assured. "Remembering the past and what you're trying to forget will help. Your past and what you're running away from must be faced in order for you to maintain peace of mind."

"Now tell me, did Elizabeth Maxwell have a boyfriend?"

"Yes. She hung around with a hippie in our commune. As I recall, I believe his name was Martin Phelpman."

"Can you remember anything or anybody else during that period of your life?"

"Just vaguely, although some people and events seem to be etched in my mind. Martin and Elizabeth and another girl we called Liz, or Lizzy who was running around with an older man."

"Do you know if this Martin and Elizabeth ever got married?"

Andrew scratched at his head. "I'm not really sure. She was young then, sixteen or seventeen, too young to marry in this state. It's hard to recall but I vaguely remember Liz going with a couple to witness a wedding in another state. I think it could have been them or maybe it was some other couple I knew at the time."

"This Liz and the older man, did they ever get married?"

"No. He stayed out of the commune. Liz would disappear for awhile, and then come back after the two did their thing."

"What thing?"

"Sex! All he was after was the free sex with Liz, her being so young. As I recall, he eventually gave her a job at his newspaper."

Andrea began to put the pieces together. She felt sure he was talking about Lizzy the elderly women working in the newspaper archives. She wondered who the old man might have been.

"What about you and Claire?" she continued, trying not to arouse any suspicion from Andrew.

"I left her. I couldn't take the pressure she was putting on me. That's when I began to drink heavily. Not wanting to be part of the high and mighty circle of people she knew and her family, one day I decided to leave, travel the country. That was the last of Claire."

Andrea looked at her watch. She had heard enough, wanting to get to her mother's office.

"I have to leave now. You get some rest and I'll see you at our next scheduled visit."

Andrew glanced at her. "Thank you, doctor. I hope the information I gave you will be helpful."

"You talking about your past is what is helpful. Bringing your past to the forefront will help you cope with life and help you with your cure."

Andrew turned toward her and smiled.

Andrea left the room and quickly walked to her mother's office. Reaching her office door, she knocked on it.

"Come in," came the muffled reply.

Andrea opened the door. "Mother," Andrea exclaimed excitedly, "I just found out some very interesting news about you. I learned you were married to somebody besides my father. He left you. Why didn't you tell me you were married to someone else before you married my father?"

Claire appeared shocked. She leaned back into her chair, carefully thinking as to how she needed to respond. Andrea waited in anticipation for her reaction.

"Well yes," she replied cautiously. "But that was somebody I knew a long time ago. It was just an unfortunate event at the time. It passed. I put it out of my mind. I didn't feel it was necessary to burden you. Forget it, honey. It was nothing."

Andrea was skeptical. She wanted to believe her but something in the back of her mind bothered her. The room was silent. Andrea watched her mother.

Andrea broke the deafening silence. "I have some more news. Some good, possibly not so good."

Claire looked up from her desk nervously. "What other news do you have?"

"Don't be upset mother, but I think I came across your ex-husband, the one who married you and left before I was born."

Claire closed her eyes. "Who could be this ex-husband of mine you think you've met?

"Andrew Simpson," Andrea replied.

"Oh no!" Claire said, "Don't tell me the Andrew Simpson admitted as a patient is same Andrew Simpson I knew so long ago? I thought he was long gone."

Andrea felt relieved, seeing her mother was taking the news lightly. "Yes and he just happens to be a patient assigned to my care. Didn't you recognize him when you went into his room the day he was admitted?"

"No Andrea I didn't. Besides so many years have passed. I'm sure I wouldn't recognize him if he came up to me and introduced himself to me."

"I suppose that is possible," Andrea commented . . . "So tell me about him," she asked, eagerly.

"Oh darling, he was just a passing fancy. Yes, we married but that was a disaster. It lasted a very short time, just a few months. After he disappeared I obtained a divorce. Anyway I didn't feel the need to burden you with that unfortunate part of my life. Besides, if your grandparents wanted you to know about my past, they would have told you. It was a closed chapter in my life."

"But mother," Andrea interjected, "he said he loved you, but you pushed him too hard. He said he couldn't handle the pressure, pressure from his job and you."

"Andrea, let's not be one sided about what you've been told or learned about me and what happened in the past. You only heard one side of the story. How many times have I told you to not judge until you hear both sides? You know better," she admonished.

Andrea blushed. She knew her mother was right. "But I do think it would be good therapy for him if you were to go to him and . . ."

Claire cut Andrea short with a stern look on her face. "No! Under no circumstances will I got into his room to meet him. I don't care to bring up that part of my past, having to rehash that mess. It was a very unpleasant experience for me."

Andrea was not prepared for the interjecting. Realizing her mother was sincere; she decided it best to drop the subject for the time being.

"There's other news," Andrea volunteered.

Claire glared at her.

"I know my uncle's name," Andrea said, smiling slightly.

"You do? What's his name? It is obvious you'll burst unless you tell me."

"Martin Phelpman," Andrea announced.

"Are you sure?" Claire questioned.

"Yes," Andrea replied, puzzled that she would question her on hearing his name. "It seems Andrew Simpson, knew this Mr. Phelpman."

Claire gave a silent sight of relief. "Martin Phelpman!" she repeated.

"Yes, Martin Phelpman and I are going to find him."

"How do you know he's still alive?" Claire questioned.

Andrea looked up at her. "I don't know. I suppose he still is alive. At least, I hope he's alive. Is he? Have you seen him?"

"I can't say," replied Claire. "This Martin Phelpman, your supposed uncle, disappeared a long time ago. I don't know anyone living in this city named Martin Phelpman."

Andrea expressed disappointment at her reply. She remained silent for a few moments, studying her mother's expression. She felt her mother was hiding something from her.

Andrea stood up.

"I have to get to my patients. You need not worry about Andrew Simpson. If you don't want to meet him, then, for my part, he won't know you're here at the center. Besides, his treatment is nearing completion. I'll probably recommend he be discharged, perhaps early next week."

Claire smiled. "Thank you, darling. It would bother me deeply having to remember that period of my life. I don't want my life complicated by the reappearance of Andrew Simpson."

Andrea walked to the office door and stepped outside. She closed the door behind her, leaving Claire to herself.

CHAPTER THIRTEEN

CLAIRE WAS RELIEVED Andrea did not know the whole story, although the revelation about events and people bothered her deeply. She thought over what Andrea had learned about Andrew and Marty. She concluded she would have to take matters in her own hands to prevent any further developments.

She picked up the phone and dialed a number. After several rings, someone answered.

"Doctor Thomason's office, may I help you?" a woman said.

"This is Doctor Maxwell at the Maxwell Rehabilitation Center. I would like to speak to Doctor Thomason."

"Yes. Please hold, Doctor Maxwell."

Claire waited. Several minutes elapsed before another voice was heard.

"Doctor Thomason speaking, how can I help you Doctor Maxwell?"

"I'm calling about our patient Mr. Andrew Simpson. Could you please tell me about his condition? I believe you are waiting for some test results to come back from the lab."

"Yes." Doctor Thomason replied. "I just received his lab report this morning and had planned to call you later. Unfortunately, he has liver cancer and it is in the terminal stages. It is only a matter of days or perhaps a couple weeks at the most."

Claire nearly dropped the phone at the revelation. She thanked Doctor Thomason and hung up the phone. She put her hands to her face.

"Oh my God!" She exclaimed aloud.

Over the shock, she picked up the phone again and dialed another number. After a few rings, the phone connected.

"This is Doctor Maxwell. Please bring Mr. Simpson's chart to my office."

She hung up the phone and waited for her request to be carried out. After a short delay, someone knocked on her door.

"Come in," she called.

The door opened and in stepped a nurse.

"Doctor, here's the chart on Mr. Simpson you requested."

The nurse walked over to Claire's desk and handed the chart to her. She was about to leave, when Claire stopped her.

"Please wait a moment while I review this chart. I may have some instructions for you."

"Yes, doctor," the nurse replied.

Claire carefully paged through Andrew's chart. Satisfied with what she was reading, she looked up at the nurse.

"Inform the admissions office Mr. Simpson has completed his treatment and is to be discharged today. I'll keep this chart and take it to medical records myself. I have to enter some notations in it."

"Yes, doctor," The nurse replied.

Claire picked up the phone again and dialed another number. After several rings, a man replied.

"Hello, Marty Fieldman speaking."

"Marty. This is Claire."

"Yes, Claire. What do you want?" he asked in a cold voice.

"I'm discharging Andrew this afternoon. Please come and get him."

Marty did not respond to her announcement. After a short delay, he asked, "Is his treatment completed? Is he cured?"

"Yes," replied Claire. "However, he will require some follow up sessions. You need to make sure he goes downtown to the annex building for his sessions. If he doesn't, he may have a relapse."

"He's only been in the center for a short time. Are you sure he's cured or you just trying to get rid of him in the fear Andrea may find out he's her father? Or is it because he might run into you?"

"He has progressed to a point he needn't be kept at the center. We need the bed. We're booked solid and patients are waiting. Please come and get him."

Claire slammed down the phone. She closed her eyes to calm herself. She remained in the posture while reviewing the events with Andrea. She was tormented; pained realizing Andrea had a right to know her father. She didn't know what to do. She was afraid of what would happen between the two of them if Andrea found out her father was alive and who he really was.

Claire's solitude was interrupted by a knock on the door and Andrea stepping into the office.

"Mother, what in the world are you doing? I just found out you are discharging Mr. Simpson. Why?"

Claire looked up at her. "His program is near completion. The remaining sessions can be accomplished at our annex downtown. We need the beds and because of the progress he is making I feel there is no harm in sending him to our annex. Besides he'll need to go there for supplemental treatments anyway. Having him start using the annex earlier fit's the bill. As I said, we need the beds."

"I wanted to work with him for a few more days," Andrea replied. "I think it's too soon for him to be discharged."

"May I remind you I control what goes on here. Besides, I think it's best for him, and everyone concerned that he's discharged, the sooner the better."

Andrea looked at her mother angrily. "Why? It's as though you're trying to get rid of him. Are you afraid he might run into you?"

Claire turned away from her. "No. There's more to Mr. Simpson's situation. I just spoke to Doctor Thomason at the Community hospital. Andrew Simpson is dying. He has terminal Cancer, and doesn't have long to live."

"Oh no!" Andrea exclaimed. "I didn't know."

Claire got up and walked over to Andrea. "Darling, it doesn't matter now. His time remaining is so short, it wouldn't matter if he reverted back to being an alcoholic. It appears, all your efforts were in vain. His cancer is so far advanced; he could die at any time."

Sizing up the situation Andrea agreed with her mother, understanding the circumstances. She had seen patients in the past experiencing similar conditions.

"I still think it would be a wonderful gesture if you went and saw him. Realizing he hasn't much time to live, wouldn't it lift his spirits if you saw him just one more time?"

Claire knew Andrea was concerned about her patients and how she took pleasure at seeing them happy.

"Please mother. It won't hurt you. You can go into his room alone. I won't interfere," Andrea pleaded.

Claire relented, "Okay, I'll do it for you. But you have to promise not to come in the room while I visit him."

Andrea made a face. "Oh Mother. He's just a patient. Go, make him happy. I'll keep out of the way."

"I will darling," she replied. "You had better get about your duties. I'll see him before he leaves the center. Just give me a little time to freshen up."

Andrea smiled. "Thanks, Mom."

She kissed her on the cheek, turned around and left the office.

Claire fretted, not knowing how she was going to handle the meeting. She walked to a small rest room adjoining her office. She looked at herself in the mirror, staring at her reflection.

"What will he say? What will he do?" she questioned, as though expecting a reply from the mirror.

She closed her eyes. "I may as well get it done."

Claire walked out of the rest room, through her office and out into the corridor. She walked to Andrew's room. She hesitated when she came to his door. Her face became flushed. She was sure this meeting would bring on an anxiety attack. Inhaling deeply, she knocked on the door and slowly opened it.

She was apprehensive of what might happen. She stepped inside the room. Andrew was sitting on the bedside chair, looking out the window.

Claire waited until the door had closed behind her before she said anything. Andrew didn't turn around to acknowledge his visitor. Claire stood for several seconds, watching him from a distance.

"Andrew?" she finally called out.

He turned around.

"Yes?" he answered. "Who is it?"

Claire walked closer to him. She was an arms span away. "It's Claire!"

Andrew stood up. Tears began streaming down his face on recognizing her.

"Claire," he said, in a choked voice. "Claire."

Claire could not contain herself. She walked over to him. The two embraced, holding one another as a loving couple would embrace after a long absence. He held her tightly.

"My God," he said. "It's so good to see you. You can't imagine how I've longed to have you back in my arms."

Claire broke away from the embrace. She stared at Andrew, wanting to get a good look at him.

"You're looking good," she said, forcing the words out.

Due to the cancer, Andrew had been steadily losing weight. His face began to become drawn. His color was pale. It was obvious the disease was taking its toll.

Andrew glanced at the floor.

"Yes. Considering what I've been through all these years. The people at this center do a good job."

"We do our best," Claire said.

Andrew looked at her questionably. "We?" he asked."

"Yes. We! I'm a doctor. Have been for many years."

Andrew studied her.

"Yes, I imagined you would do something with your life. I'm happy for you."

"And you?" Claire asked.

Andrew turned around, walked to the window and stared out. "I need not tell you about me. My life fell apart. I wasn't cut out to live the life I started with you. I couldn't handle life and what it had in store for me."

"So, what will you do now?" she asked.

He turned around. "I'm not sure. If it wasn't for Mr. Fieldman, I wouldn't be here today. I suppose my future is in his hands. He's a good person."

"Do you plan to continue working for him?"

"I don't know. I guess I'll try but I'm not feeling too well. I have this nagging ache that doesn't want to go away. Doctors I've seen in the past said there was nothing they can do about the pain. It slows me down a bit but I'll manage. I always have."

Claire looked away. She knew it was the cancer eating away at his insides. She wanted to help, although at a loss for what to do.

Andrew walked to the chair, moving as though he was exhausted. He sat down. "You still look as beautiful as you did back when we were together."

Claire blushed. Recalling the short time they were together.

"I did love you, Andrew," she said. "We had some good times, some good friends. Then you left. You just left me." There was anger in her voice.

"I know," Andrew replied with sadness in his voice. "I suppose you divorced me and got on with your life?"

"What did you expect?" Claire said. "Was I to hold on to an empty dream?"

Andrew managed a smile. "Yes. You're a Maxwell, one of the mighty Maxwells."

Claire gave him a stern glance.

"It's okay," he quickly responded. "I blame myself for all that's happened between us. Don't let it bother you."

Claire relaxed. "You don't fault me?"

"No, of course not. I couldn't cope, so I dropped out and eventually buried myself, my problems in alcohol."

"Is there anything I can do for you?" Claire asked.

Andrew looked at her.

"Yes. It would be nice to see you once in awhile. I mean, professionally. I'm sure your husband wouldn't like you seeing me, knowing we were married once."

"Oh. You needn't worry about him. He's not around anymore," she said, avoiding his eyes.

Andrew perked up. "You're not married?"

"I'm not married now."

"That's wonderful."

Claire smiled. She realized he was trying to re-establish a long lost link between the two of them.

Suddenly Andrew bent over on the chair and grimaced.

"Andrew, what's the matter?" Claire asked quickly.

He held fast, not responding immediately. Several minutes passed before he replied.

"It's alright now. I get these attacks once in awhile. It'll pass."

Claire walked over to the bed, picked up the remote control module and pushed one of the buttons.

A few seconds later, a nurse came running into the room. Claire walked over to the nurse and spoke to her. Andrew did not hear what she had said.

The nurse departed the room. Several minutes passed. She returned with a syringe.

Claire picked up the syringe, evacuated the air from it and walked over to Andrew.

"This will ease the pain," she said.

Andrew did not resist. Claire stuck the needle into his arm, pressing the plunger, forcing the liquid into his veins. She extracted the needle and rubbed his arm where the puncture was made. Putting the expended syringe back on the tray, she instructed the nurse to leave the room.

"I think you had better lie down on the bed," she instructed.

Andrew got up from the chair and laid down. He looked up at Claire.

"It's bad, isn't it?"

She was on the verge of tears. Suddenly the door opened. Claire turned toward the door. Marty stepped inside.

"It's about time," Marty said with a frown.

Claire gave Marty a stern look. Andrew glanced up at Marty. The drug began to affect him.

"Martin," he said, as he closed his eyes, falling into a restful sleep.

Claire looked at Marty, with wide eyes.

"He called you Martin!" Claire exclaimed.

Marty looked sheepishly at her.

"He called you Martin. You must have told him something about me and Andrea while he was working in your junkyard."

"The only thing I told him was my new name. Nothing more. He didn't recognize me or remember me until I told him the name I went by back then.

Claire was furious. "Are you sure you didn't tell him about Andrea? Oh, God forbid. He can't know about her. Not yet. I need more time to think things out. I've paid you and Lizzy to keep this from happening. Why don't you just leave me and Andrea alone?"

"Stop it Claire!" Marty yelled. "It doesn't matter if he does know her, now or later. What matter is, what you're going to do about telling him. Are you going to carry on the charade or let what eventually happens take place?"

Claire looked at Marty with pleading eyes, knowing too well he'd be intent when there was something he deemed necessary to do. It was obvious his concern for Andrew and Andrea was sincere. He felt compelled to see that the two were brought together. Knowing Marty would be reluctant to forgo his intent, she hoped he would see her side of the situation and allows her time to plan how to accomplish his desire.

"I know it's sudden," he said, "a lot to ask of you. But please, for Andrea's sake, don't take too long. Doctor Thomason called me this morning. You know his condition, how serious it is. I'd be disappointed if he passed away not knowing he has a daughter."

"I will, just let me collect my thoughts. I spoke with Doctor Thomason a few minutes ago. From the sudden pain he experienced, it would be best if he were transferred back to the hospital. At lease he'll be off the streets and able to get pain medication."

Marty glanced down at Andrew. "Do you really think so?"

"Yes," replied Claire.

"As you wish Claire, but make sure he's in a private room I'll see to his expenses."

Claire could see Marty was saddened by the turn of events.

"Is there any hope? Can he come out of this?" Marty asked. "Perhaps there's some new medication that can combat his disease. We could have Doctor Thomason recommend a specialist.

Claire turned around with her back toward the two men. She fought back the tears.

"No," she said. "There's no known operation or cure for his condition. He's going to die. All we can do is make his pain more bearable. For someone to be there for him, comfort him. There's little we can do here."

Marty walked over to Andrew and picked up his hand. He patted it. "I'll be here for you Andrew," he said.

Marty looked at Claire. "What about you? Are you going to be there for him?"

"I don't know. I need time to think. I just now got up the courage to see him. Don't push me. You've done enough damage for now."

Marty looked at her doubtfully.

"You had better make arrangements to have him transferred to the hospital," he said.

Claire walked over to the night stand and picked up the phone receiver and dialed a number.

"Community General Hospital admissions. Mrs. Wilcox speaking," a voice announced.

"Mrs. Wilcox, this is Doctor Claire Maxwell, of the Maxwell Center. Please make arrangements to have a Mr. Andrew Simpson transferred from our facility to your hospital. He's to be put into a private room. Mr. Fieldman will be there to sign the necessary admission papers."

Mrs. Wilcox obtained some preliminary information from Claire. Completed with the conversation, Claire hung up the phone, while looking at Marty.

"You need to go to the hospital and take care of the admission papers."

Marty nodded. He walked to the door, opened it and stepped into the corridor, closing the door behind him.

Claire remained in the room. She looked down at Andrew. He was at peace.

"Oh Andrew," she said. "Why did you have to come back?" Everything was perfect until now. Why didn't you stay away?"

She contemplated the bazaar situation and tried to figure out how she was going to tell him about Andrea. Suddenly the door to the room flung open. Andrea stepped into the room.

"Mother, what's happening? I just found you're transferring Mr. Simpson to Community General Hospital. Why? I thought you were discharging him?"

"His condition is far worse off than expected."

Andrea looked shocked.

"I just gave him an injection for the pain. He's in stage four with the cancer."

Claire walked over to Andrea and put her arms around her.

"Mr. Fieldman went to the hospital to make arrangements for him to be admitted. I know how easy it is to get close to a patient. I've done so in the past, believe me, I know how you feel and what agony you're going through."

Andrea managed a smile. "Thanks, mother. I appreciate your concern."

Claire broke away from the embrace. "We had better see about getting his personal items gathered."

Claire walked over to the closet, opened the door and began removing clothes. The two busied themselves getting Andrew ready for the transfer to the hospital.

As they worked, Andrew began to stir. Claire realized he would soon be awake. She did not want Andrew to see her in the room while Andrea was there. She was afraid Andrea would inadvertently call her mother. She walked over to Andrea and tapped her on the shoulder.

Looking at her watch, Claire whispered, “Darling, I have to tend to a patient. You continue here. I’ll see you later.”

Andrea nodded.

Claire swiftly made her exit from the room. As the door closed behind her, Andrew woke up. He rolled over in the bed toward the direction of the subdued noises he was hearing, and glanced at Andrea.

“Hi,” he said. “Who are you?”

Andrea appeared startled by the sudden sound of his voice. She walked over to him.

“I’m your doctor. Remember?” she replied.

He continued staring at her without speaking, attempting to recall Andrea. He began to recognize his surroundings.

“You’re so beautiful,” he said.

“I see from that comment, you’re starting to come out of your haze. How do you feel?” she asked.

“A little groggy! Everything’s fuzzy. What happened?”

“You were given something to ease your pain. The medication will make you a little disorientated but that will pass in time.”

Andrew did not reply. He continued looking at Andrea. He watched as she went about folding his clothes and placing his personal articles in a plastic bag. She set his coat over the back of the chair.

“What are you doing?” Andrew questioned.

Without look at him, she replied, “I’m getting your things together. We’re going to transfer you to Community General Hospital. You’re very ill and need the attention of medical doctors. We aren’t able to handle your condition here at the center.”

“Will I see you again?”

“No,” she replied. “I don’ believe it would be possible for me to come see you at the hospital. I have many patients I must see each day here at the center but you needn’t worry. The people at the hospital will give you good care.”

Andrew looked away from her, saddened by her response.

“Where’s Martin?” he suddenly asked.

“Martin who?”

“The man who brought me here.”

"You must mean Marty, not Martin. Marty Fieldman."

"Yes. I guess," he replied.

"He went to the hospital to make arrangements to have you admitted as a patient,"

Andrew rolled over onto his back and closed his eyes.

Andrea walked over to the window and looked outside, pondering the weather. She sighed, as she noticed clouds forming again. As she continued to peer out the window, an ambulance pulled up to main entrance.

"I see your hospital transportation is here," she said, turning toward Andrew.

He glanced at her without saying anything.

Andrea walked over to the phone and picked up the receiver. She dialed a number and waited for a response.

"This is Doctor Andrea Maxwell. Mr. Simpson is being transferred to the hospital. Have the paramedics come directly up to his room as soon as they arrive. She hung up the phone.

Several minutes passed, when a knock came on the door. Andrea walked to the door and opened it. Two paramedics stood in the hallway with the gurney from the ambulance.

"Is this Mr. Simpson's room?" one of the paramedics inquired.

Andrea nodded. The two men rolled the gurney into the room, placing it next to Andrew's bed. Carefully, after adjusting the gurney to the height of the bed, they maneuvered him onto it.

Andrea watched in silence. She walked over to the chair and picked up his clothing and the plastic bag containing his personal articles.

"These are his things," she said, handing the pile of articles to one of the paramedics.

He took the clothing and bag from Andrea and placed it on the foot of the gurney.

Assured Andrew was secured on the gurney the paramedics rolled it out into the corridor, letting the door to the room close behind them. Andrea stayed behind in the room. As they began pushing the gurney down the corridor, Andrea rushed out of the room with Andrews' coat.

"His coat. He'll need his coat," she called out.

The two stopped the gurney as Andrea walked up to it. She placed the coat over Andrew. He looked up at her and smiled. The gurney once again began down the hallway. Andrea decided to walk alongside it as they made their way through the center.

"Wait!" Andrew suddenly called out in a choked voice.

The two paramedics appeared disturbed by the sudden request. Reluctantly they stopped the gurney, glancing at Andrea.

Andrew, with difficulty searched through the pockets of his coat. He withdrew an envelope and handed it to Andrea.

"Here," he said.

Andrea reached down and took the envelope from him and put it into her smock pocket.

Andrew motioned for her to come close to him. Andrea bent down toward Andrew, realizing he wanted to say something.

"Tell her I still love her. Always have."

Andrea swallowed hard, fighting back tears.

"I will," she said.

The journey through the center continued. Reaching the main entrance, the paramedics carefully pushed the gurney into the ambulance, got in and took off down the driveway. Andrea watched as it disappeared among busy traffic. Several tears trickled down her cheek.

She stood a few moments until she was over the loss of her patient. Having recovered, she turned and walked back into the lobby. She was greeted by her mother, who was watching through the glass doors.

As she passed through the door, Claire stopped her.

"Darling, it's for the best. At least he'll be comfortable in the hospital. They'll give him the best of care until the end."

Andrea was solemn. "Yes, I suppose you're right. There is nothing else to do for him. If you don't mind I would like to be alone now."

"Yes dear," Claire replied.

Andrea walked to her office. Reaching it, she opened the door and stepped inside. Closing the door behind her, she walked to the desk chair and sat down. She could not get Andrew out of her mind. Something about him bothered her.

Andrea sat in silence, going over the events of the morning. Remembering the envelope Andrew had given her, she reached into her smock and withdrew it. Studying the envelope, she wondered why he had given it to her.

Slowly, she opened the envelope and withdrew a photograph, the only item in it. To her amazement, it was the picture of her mother he cherished. A smile came to her face as she recalled what her mother had told her about Andrew.

"Poor fellow," she said. "You do still love her, even though you two didn't make it together."

Returning the picture to the envelope, she haphazardly placed it into her smock pocket. She made a mental note to show it to her mother.

CHAPTER FOURTEEN

MICHAEL CONTINUED HOLDING Lizzy in his arms as she cried. He felt sorrow for her, knowing the years she had lived were in torment. He understood the shame and disgrace she would have had to experience. The denial by people she worked with in trying to name Mr. Maxwell as the father of her illegitimate child.

Although Michael was loved and reared by the Maxwell family, he had often wondered what had happened to his natural parents. Whenever he would bring up the subject, they would evade the issue. In time, Michael quit asking about them, being content with the life he was living.

Lizzy ceased crying. She looked up at him. "Michael, can you ever forgive me for abandoning you?"

Although the years as a reporter had toughened Michael, he was still compassionate and understanding. He knew sometimes people were victims of society, their fate controlled by others.

"I understand what you went through back then. How can I condemn you, considering the position you were put in. Mr. Maxwell backed you into a corner, forced to do what you didn't want to do."

"Are you sure?" she asked again.

Michael looked into her eyes. She tried to look away, in shame, but Michael gently held her chin, preventing her from turning. Reaching with one hand, he brushed away the tears from her face.

"Yes. Lizzy, I'm sure. I was taught to love my fellow man, regardless of the situation. It isn't for me to judge people for what they did in the past."

"Everything will be fine," Michael said softly.

Several minutes passed before she could bring herself to stop crying. Lizzy broke away from the embrace, walked to the parlor and sat down on a sofa. Michael followed, sitting next to her.

Michael studied Lizzy's features. Although he had seen her many times at the newspaper, he had never paid close attention to her. Time had been good to her. She had aged graciously and was still an attractive woman despite the spent years of her life. The two continued looking at one another without saying a word. To Michael, it became a golden moment in their lives.

"How did you find out? Who told you about me? Was it Marty? Claire?"

"It was Claire, but only after much prodding, and I suppose because of the events beginning to unfold. She reluctantly, gave in and told me the whole story, about you, Mr. Maxwell, Marty, and Andrew. Although she was hesitant in saying, she did confirm your story, about you being my mother."

"Then you know? You know about Andrew Simpson, about him being Andrea's father?"

Yes," Michael replied. "I know, but Andrea doesn't. I haven't told her. Neither has her mother. I'm not certain telling her would be such a good idea. I don't think Andrea would be able to handle that kind of news, at least not now."

"She has a right to know. Just as much right knowing about her father as you did in finding about me. If Andrea ever found out about her father, and that you knew him, it would be a disaster for the two of you. What would she think? How would she react?"

Michael looked away, saddened, knowing she was right.

"It's true love's ways, Michael."

"True love's ways?" he questioned.

"It's a phrase from a Buddy Holly song we used to listen to a lot back then. A phrase he learned from his wife. If you love someone, your actions not words, reveals your true love."

"I love her. It is going to ruin everything her knowing about you being my mother and her grandfather being my father."

"Believe me, Michael, if you keep this from her, you'll live your life in misery, always fearing the day to come when she'll eventually find out. You can't live your life a lie. You'll just have to face the fact that it would not be proper to marry her. You have to tell her."

"I know," he said. "As much as it would hurt me, I realize I must. I'm sure Claire would be elated over me telling Andrea. Claire was never happy about me getting close to Andrea."

Michael sighed. "Well then, it's settled. I'm sure she won't welcome the news. I'll just have to let the chips fall where they may."

"Everything will work out," Lizzy said. "Believe me, you'll have a much better life ahead of you if you're truthful. Please, don't hide anything. No matter what the cost. I should know, having lived the lie and suffering all these years because of it."

Michael knew Lizzy's meaning. He had seen countless number of people, their lives and careers ruined by something they had kept secret from their past. Events revealed by newspaper reports, events not too pleasant.

"It'll take time to get use to you being my mother. If you don't mind, I would be more comfortable calling you Lizzy."

"I don't mind Michael. I would be happy just knowing you realize I am your mother."

Michael stood up. "I must be leaving. I have to see Andrea and tell her the bad news."

Lizzy could hear the hurt in his voice. She was saddened. She turned away from him. She didn't want to look into his eyes.

Michael walked to the front door. She followed close behind. He opened the door, but before he stepped outside, he bent down and kissed Lizzy on the cheek.

"I'll be back," he said.

He returned to his car, got in and started the engine. He began to drive off when Lizzy suddenly called out. "Wait Michael!" she yelled. "I've got to be truthful with you." She was crying.

He didn't hear her . . . Michael was preoccupied while he traveled the streets, making his way back to the rehabilitation center. Reaching the front entrance, he stopped the car, got out and walked to the front door. Passing through the lobby, he headed directly to Andrea's office.

Reaching her office, he knocked and opened the door without being invited in. Andrea glanced up from behind her desk.

"Michael," she said happily.

He walked over to her and gave her a peck on the cheek.

"What kind of kiss is that?" she asked, as he sat on an overstuffed chair adjacent to her desk.

Michael managed a smile. "I have something to tell, you you'll find very disturbing. I don't know where to start, how to tell you."

Andrea look at him, puzzled. "What news?"

"I just discovered who your uncle is"

Andrea stood up excitedly. "I already know. I found out from an old boyfriend of mothers. The only thing is, no one knows where he is."

Michael looked at Andrea questioningly. "What do you mean? You've already met him."

"What?" Andrea exclaimed. "I haven't met anyone named Martin Phelpman."

"Andrea, he doesn't go by Martin Phelpman anymore."

"He doesn't? What name is he using now?" Michael cleared his throat. "Marty Fieldman."

"What? Michael, what are you saying?"

"Marty Fieldman is your uncle. He was married to your Aunt Elizabeth.

"The same Marty Fieldman who has been sponsoring Mr. Simpson"

"Yes," Michael replied.

Andrea could barely believe her ears.

"Lizzy told me," Michael said, in a subdued voice. "The woman you met in archives. She told me the whole story."

"The whole story? What does that mean?"

"There's much more, most unpleasant for all concerned. You, me and your mother."

"You? There's something I don't know about you? Is it bad, Michael?"

"Yes, very unpleasant. I just found out that Lizzy is my biological mother."

Andrea's sat back down, astonished at what he said.

"It can't be all that bad, Michael. So now you know who your real mother is."

"No. I've gotten over the shock of finding out about her. That isn't what's so bad. What isn't so pleasant is finding out about my father."

"You know who your father is? Who is he?"

Michael looked away from her. He feared telling her.

"It's your grandfather. Mark Maxwell."

"Oh my lord, Michael! Don't say that. Please don't say that," Andrea said her voice cracking as she spoke.

Michael was saddened. "It's true," he continued. "What's worse, your mother knew about Lizzy and your grandfather and me. She kept it a secret all these years."

Andrea got up from her chair and walked over to Michael. As she sat down beside him, the envelope partially hanging out of her smock pocket fell to the floor.

Michael watched as the tears rolled down her cheeks. Tears began welling up in his eyes. He fought them forming.

"Under the circumstances, there is no way we can marry," he said.

She managed to nod in agreement, continuing to sob.

Michael remained silent, as did Andrea. The two sat without speaking for several minutes. Michael thought over the situation, searching deep down inside himself. He could not bear to lose Andrea. He reached over and held her hand.

The two embraced and kissed for what they felt would be their last kiss. He reached up and ran his hand through her long, silky hair.

"I guess we'll get over this hurdle," he said, as he held her in his arms.

She looked up at him, managing a smile among her tears. "You bet we will."

Michael glanced down at the floor, noticing the envelope that had fallen out of her pocket. Reaching down, he picked it up.

"You must have dropped this," he said, handing it to her.

She looked at the envelope, and forced a laugh. Michael looked to her in surprise. "What is it?"

"You've got to see this," she said. "It's a picture of mother when she was young. I've never seen a picture of her like this one."

Andrea opened the envelope and took out the photograph, handing it to Michael. He took the picture and looked at it. He managed to chuckle.

"Looks a lot like you, doesn't she?"

Andrea gave him a light tap on the arm. "Look at the weird clothes she's wearing, and the beads in her hair. How can you say I look like her?"

"She does, without all the beads and the weird clothes. Look at her face and the long hair. You two could pass as twins or sisters."

The two sat looking at the old photograph.

"Where did you get this? Michael asked.

"From an old boyfriend my mother once dated. In fact, they were once married, but it didn't last. Mother divorced him. She told me it was just a passing fancy. She said the marriage wouldn't have lasted anyway."

Michael's face became solemn. "I didn't know he was married before. Who was this boyfriend?" he asked.

"You'll find this hard to believe. It was Andrew Simpson. The very Andrew Simpson here at the center, one of my patients," she replied.

"Oh no!" said Michael. "Not him."

Andrea appeared shaken by his sudden exclamation.

"What is it?" Andrea asked.

"It's Andrew Simpson. He's part of the puzzle."

"What?" she asked, worriedly.

"Andrea, Andrew Simpson is your father."

Andrea glared at Michael. "No he isn't! My father died in Vietnam. Mother said Andrew Simpson was just an old boyfriend she married and divorced. He can't be my father. I refuse to believe he's my father."

"Andrea," Michael said with a stern voice. "Listen to me. Your mother told me, and Lizzy confirmed he was your father. I believe her, them. Why would they lie?"

"No! This is too much. I can't accept it. He's an alcoholic, a nothing. I can't believe this. Tell me, Michael. It has to be a lie."

Michael had dropped a verbal bomb on her, revealing what she did not want to accept. He got up from the couch and walked to the bookshelf, evading Andrea's eyes.

The room once again grew silent. Andrea got up and paced the floor.

"I can't take this," she said, breaking the silence. "You're ruining everything! Why did you have to find these things out? Why couldn't you have left things as they were?"

Michael did not reply, knowing she would have to eventually accept the facts.

She continued to pace the floor with a worried look on her face.

Michael glanced at her. "Under the circumstances, let's forget dinner tonight. I think it best if I left you alone to work things out."

"Yes. I need to be alone so I can sort out this quagmire."

Michael walked over to her. Reaching her, he was about to give her a kiss, but she turned her head away. He backed off.

He walked to the door and opened it. "I'll see you later," he said, looking in her direction. She didn't reply. Michael left himself out of the office, leaving Andrea to her solitude. It pained him deeply having to be the barer of bad news.

CHAPTER FIFTEEN

THE DOOR HAVING closed, Andrea shouted. "Damn! Damn! What's happening all of a sudden? My world is falling apart."

Returning to her desk, she was about to pick up the phone when there was a sudden knock on the door. Not in the mood to see anyone, she reluctantly called out, "Come in."

There was a slight delay.

"Come in!" she called again.

The door slowly opened. Marty looked into the office at Andrea.

"May I come in?" he asked.

Andrea was disturbed by his sudden appearance, barely able to form the words, she replied. "Ah . . . Yes, come in."

Marty slowly stepped into the office, carefully making his way to the overstuffed chair, limping more than usual.

He sat down appearing exasperated.

"Andrea?" he asked, "Do you know who I am?"

She could not bring herself to look directly at him feeling inwardly guilty, knowing how the Maxwell family had treated him.

"Yes. You're my Uncle Marty. You were Elizabeth's husband."

"It's life," Marty said. "Unfortunate as the situation is, you're a part of my world."

He got up from the chair and walked over to her and gave her a hug. Andrea did not respond at first. The tears once again began trailing down her face. Relenting, she hugged Marty.

Marty began to cry. They were tears of joy. Of being rejoined with a loved one he was unwillingly forced to stay away from for many years.

"I love you," he said. "I was wrong for staying away from you all these years. I should have done something about this matter a long time ago. You're like a daughter I never had."

Andrea remained silent. She clung to him as she would a father.

Studying his face through her tears, she removed one arm from around him and gently put her hand to his face, tracing the many scars.

"You loved Elizabeth very much, didn't you?" she asked.

Marty removed his arms from around her. Reaching into his pocket withdrew a hanky and wiped the tears from his face.

"Yes, I did love Elizabeth very much. This limp I have and the scars you see, these are my punishment for what I did to her, for being the cause of her death."

"It was unjust," Andrea said. "No one should have to bear such punishment. I'm ashamed of the Maxwell family. We shouldn't have made you go through life carrying this burden."

Marty expressed surprise. "No, Andrea. It wasn't your fault. You have no need to feel guilty."

"That's unacceptable," she said, "I'm part of the Maxwell family. The mighty Maxwell Empire! We were responsible for your suffering."

"Please don't think that way. I was solely responsible. No one held me back or kept me from seeing the family. I alone elected to keep my distance."

"So why now? Why all of a sudden did you decide to step forward?"

Marty returned to the overstuffed chair beside her desk. "I'm afraid," he started, "I stirred up a hornets nest. I didn't intend to, but something had to be done about Andrew."

Andrea knew what was coming. She braced herself for what Marty was going to say.

She held her breath, attempting to find the courage to ask him. Finally, slowly exhaling she asked, "Is Andrew Simpson my father?"

"Yes," he replied.

He repositioned himself on the chair and began to tell Andrea what took place so long ago. She listened intently.

Three quarter of an hour passed by the time Marty had finished his tale. Andrea was horrified. The story about Michael, Marty, Elizabeth, and Andrew was retold just as Michael had learned earlier in the day from Lizzy.

"Why did mother, grandfather . . . why did they keep all this from me?" she asked.

Marty shrugged his shoulders.

"I guess since I chose to keep out of the scene, they saw reason to tell you about me. You have to realize the Maxwells were a powerful family, very influential. They went out of their way to keep scandals concerning them away from public scrutiny. I knew as much and felt it best to keep quiet. When I was a young man, at the time I was with Elizabeth and after her death, I was afraid of what could happen to me."

"Happen to you. Like what?" Andrea asked.

"Being killed!"

"What!" Andrea exclaimed.

"Yes, killed. There was something that only your grandfather and mother is aware of."

"There's more?"

"Yes," he replied, hesitantly, looking away from her. "You see, your grandfather paid me off. He gave me a substantial amount of money to keep quiet and disappear. That is, to stay away from Claire, you and even Michael. That's why I changed my name. I left the city and started to squander the money. A couple years later, and with the remaining money I returned and with a partner, started a business."

"So then, why didn't Lizzy say something? She had just as much right, being Michael's mother."

Marty cleared his throat. "I'm afraid you and Michael may have been told an untruth. I just spoke to Lizzy on the phone. I had to get over here before Michael said anything to you, but I saw him getting into his car, so I surmise he probably already spoke to you."

"An untruth? About what?" she asked.

"I came here to clear up a deception. What Michael may have told you earlier, before I arrived, has a flaw in it. The story Lizzy told

Michael. This is the reason I'm here now. To get the whole mess straightened out. I don't intend to go on and live the rest of my life with this lie. You don't deserve being punished for what I did, what Lizzy did, or your mothers' selfishness."

"What deception?" Andrea cautiously asked.

"The deception is what Lizzy told Michael. True, she is Michael's mother, but that's the extent of it. She was ashamed of a lie she told him and wants him to know the truth. I didn't know she told Michael Mr. Maxwell was his father and is the reason I'm here. There are things in the past that we did that should have never taken place."

"We?" Andrea questioned.

"Lizzy and me."

"Do you still know her?"

"Yes. I've known her for a long time."

"There's more to the story then?" asked Andrea.

"Yes," Marty answered. "Your grandfather paid Lizzy a handsome sum to keep quiet, although she did so reluctantly. It scarred him when she told him she was going to have his baby. She was just a teenager then, underage. You can imagine the scandal. Since she refused to have an abortion, he told her to disappear. He said she would always have a job at the paper and he would take care of her as long as she kept quiet and did as he asked. He stopped seeing her, returning to the security of the Maxwell household."

"Lizzy took the money and did just what he had wanted. After having the baby, about a year later she went back to him. I don't know what transpired, but it must have frightened Mr. Maxwell. She apparently was convincing, because he gave her more money, but this time, only on the condition she gave up the baby and kept quiet about the whole affair. It seems this time he had his ducks in order."

"You knew this and didn't say anything? Andrea asked.

"Yes, but only part of the story. Exploiting the Maxwells was fair game. They had the pie and we wanted a piece of it."

"You used Elizabeth?"

"No," Marty retorted. "I loved Elizabeth. Believe me. I loved her very much. No, these event took place after Elizabeth died."

Andrea backed off. She could see Marty was sincere when it came to Elizabeth. "What happened next?" she asked.

"After Lizzy gave up the child and Elizabeth's death, in our grief, the two of us got together. It wasn't a new thing with us. Lizzy had strong feelings toward me, but wouldn't say anything while she was having a fling with Mr. Maxwell."

"You were going to bed with her?"

"Yes."

"Did my mother know about you and Lizzy?"

"Yes. She didn't care. She was wrapped up with you."

"You moved in with Lizzy?"

"Yes. I moved in with her two years after Elizabeth's death. Very few people knew because we were discrete. We were afraid if Mr. Maxwell knew, then the funds would dry up. When the accident happened and after I got out of the hospital, I disappeared for a short time until things quieted down. When I returned and moved in with Lizzy, I changed my name. Mr. Maxwell never knew, but your mother did. She was aware I was living with Lizzy, but didn't say anything to your grandfather."

"Then my grandfather was being blackmailed all these years?"

"Well I suppose you could call it a mutual blackmail, but then your mother turned the tables on us."

"My mother was involved?"

"Yes, but I wouldn't say she was being blackmailed, although she did pay Lizzy to keep quiet, but that was her own doing. Mr. Maxwell told Claire to take care of Lizzy. He told her she was a dedicated and faithful employee and no matter what happened to him, she was to remain on the paper and get raises and bonuses for being a long time employee. He felt so strongly about it, he even put it in his will that Lizzy be taken care of and to what extent."

"He told Lizzy what he had commanded and is one reason she continued to keep quiet all these years. The other reason is because your mother told Lizzy she would go to the authorities and claim she was being blackmailed should she say anything."

"Does Michael know these things?" Andrea asked.

"No. Lizzy was forced to tell Michael a half truth because of your mother. You might say Lizzy was the one being blackmailed, although being paid to be blackmailed."

Marty stood up and limped to the office window. Andrea watched him, wondering about the deception.

"What about the rest of the story?"

He hesitated answering.

"What are these deceptions, half truths?" Andrea demanded.

"Lizzy, Elizabeth and I were close friends back then," he replied. "Living a commune was different, a different society. Love was free, uninhabited. At first there was no real pairing off, so to speak. I made love to any girl who would have me. It was the times. Then one day Lizzy came to me and told me she was pregnant. I asked her who the father was. She laughed."

"Laughed?"

"Yes. She laughed. She said it didn't matter, that she had a plan. She told me she was going to claim Mr. Maxwell as the father and bleed him as much as she could, even though he was not the father."

Andrea perked up. "He's not Michael's father?"

"That's right."

Andrea stood up.

Marty turned around. "It's true. Lizzy told me Mr. Maxwell was very careful, always wearing a condom when he had sex with her, which really wasn't that often. She was already pregnant by the time she started having an affair with Mr. Maxwell. She told me she was going to use the situation to her advantage and claim the condom broke. She said his real father left the commune when she told him she was pregnant and hasn't been heard of since."

"You mean Michael isn't my uncle?"

"I can assure you, your grandfather is not Michael's father. I suppose you could call him your step-uncle since Mr. Maxwell adopted him."

"But Michael said she had a birth certificate to prove he was Michael's son."

"The certificate is forged. Back then, we knew people who worked in the hospital. It was easy to get a blank birth certificate. After getting a blank, she put Michael's foot and fingerprints on it, copied all the information from the original and forged the doctors' signature. Since each birth certificate had a serial number on it, the one that was forged is recorded as missing which means should it turn up it would be voided."

"Even though Lizzy tried to claim Mr. Maxwell as the father, when pressured, Lizzy told the truth although Mr. Maxwell went to his grave not knowing he wasn't Michael's father. When your grandfather passed away, Lizzy went to your mother and told her everything. Your mother, not wanting any scandal, told Lizzy she'd pay her to keep the information to herself. When Michael and Andrea became involved with one another and planned to wed, your mother conned Lizzy into revealing to Michael, Mr. Maxwell was his father, let the cat our of the bag so to speak. She told her if she didn't do it, she would go to the authorities and claim she was being blackmailed by Lizzy. This is the part I wasn't aware of. In her remorse and out of love for Michael, she called me and explained what has transpired, asking me to intercede before Michael could say anything to you about what she told him."

Andrea remained silent.

"I'm truly sorry for the pain you've suffered because of the lies you've been told. I only hope you can find forgiveness in your heart."

"What about Andrew Simpson?" she asked again, wanting to be sure this part of the story was true. "Is he my real father?"

Yes, Andrea," he quietly replied. "Andrew Simpson is your real father."

"What happened to him? Why hasn't he come forward to see me? Why did he stay away?"

"I honestly don't know why he decided to stay away from Claire and the Maxwell family. Andrew left before you were born. Your mother didn't know she was pregnant at the time he left her."

Andrea gave Marty a strange look.

"Does this mean Andrew doesn't know I'm his daughter?"

"He doesn't know," Marty replied.

Andrea gasped. "Oh my god! Why didn't my mother tell me about Andrew being my father? Why did you withhold this information from me? Why didn't you come forward before now?"

Marty was ashamed to answer.

"Marty? Why?"

"Out of love," he replied. "Your mother loves you deeply. She didn't want anything to come in the way of your happiness, your success. With Andrew out of the picture, she didn't see the need to upset you with that unpleasant part of her life. Neither of us knew what became of Andrew and what kind of life he was living. Since Andrew wasn't around, I can see your mothers rational in not telling you about him. Knowing about Andrew couldn't have done anything for you while you were growing up."

"Why all of a sudden did you decide to tell me about Andrew?"

"Because he suddenly showed up and he's dying. It's not right for a man not to know he has a daughter. He needs to see you, Andrea. He needs to know about you. Will you go see him?"

"Yes," She said. "I'll go see him in time, but first I have to settle a few things with my mother."

Marty stood up. "Well, I hope you don't take too long. Andrew doesn't have much time to live. He could die anytime. I just came from the hospital. He doesn't look good. Doctor Thomason told me it was only a matter of days."

"I'll see him as soon as I can," Andrea assured.

Marty got up and walked toward the door. "I don't expect you to be happy with me. Please forgive me for not telling you sooner. The timing wasn't right, now it is. I wouldn't blame you if you didn't care to see me ever again."

Andrea gave him a blank look. "I'm sure I'll get over what you did, but it will take some time."

Marty opened the door and made his exit, leaving Andrea alone in her office. She picked up the phone and dialed her mother's extension. "Mother, this is Andrea. I need to talk to you right away."

She hung up the phone and waited. Several minutes passed. Claire knocked on the door, opened it and stepped inside the office. "Andrea, you sounded urgent. What is it darling?"

"Put a lid on it mother!" Andrea said, coldly, cutting her short.

Claire looked at her in surprise, quickly sitting down.

"Mother. What you kept from me all these years about Andrew Simpson, my father, is inexcusable."

Claire tried to interrupt.

"No!" Andrea shouted. "You have to hear me out. Are you so selfish, so self-centered that you can't bring yourself to forgive people for their actions? Is the Maxwell family so above life, we're beyond life, living apart from it, enclosed in an invisible shell for all to see but not touch? I could have had a father and an uncle, but because of you, my grandparents, these pleasures, joys of life were forbidden to me. Now I know about my father, I know my uncle. What Uncle Marty did, you and the Maxwell family forced him to do makes me ashamed to be part of the Maxwell family."

"Andrea!" Claire pleaded. "You were too young to understand. It was all for you. We wanted the best for you."

Andrea shouted, "My father is in the hospital dying! How can you be so cold, so unsympathetic? There was love between the two of you at one time, because I wouldn't be here if it wasn't so. Why did you do it?"

Claire looked at the floor guiltily. "Andrew could never be a Maxwell," Claire said quietly. "He was weak. It was just as well he left me. You're better off because of it."

Andrea glared at her mother. "That's a lame excuse mother! Lizzy was being blackmailed and you were part of it. To force a mother to give up a child is inexcusable. Why did grandfather do it? Why did you keep this from me all these years?"

"It was for your own good we did what we did," Claire replied. "And for that matter, Michaels own good too."

"What about the lie concerning Michael? Did you know he's not grandfather's child?"

Claire didn't respond.

"Did you know about Michael?"

Claire looked up at Andrea. "Darling, he's not of good stock. Lizzy was a harlot. She doesn't even know for sure who Michael's father is. Michael isn't Maxwell material. Yes, I knew what was going on. I would have paid ten times the amount to keep things as they were."

"You helped perpetrate this lie. You paid Lizzy to tell Michael, she and grandfather were his parents. Didn't you?"

"Yes," Claire replied.

"Is that why you were opposed to me dating him? Why you were always cold when he was around you, because he's Lizzy's son?"

"Yes."

"That's why you never took to Michael. You kept all this from me, concocting the story with the help of Lizzy that my grandfather was his father. You knew this would be the end of our relationship, and the wedding."

Claire did not say anything.

"I think you had better leave my office," Andrea said, disturbed her mother confirmed what Marty had told her.

Claire got up. Without looking at Andrea, she walked to the door, opened it and stepped out, closing the door behind her.

Andrea canceled her remaining sessions for the day. She got into her car and drove to the private club Michael frequented, knowing he would be there. Arriving at the club, she quickly got out of the car and handed the keys to the parking valet. She ran to the entrance, passing through the door as the doorman opened it for her.

She searched the tables and booths, noticing Michael in one of the booths.

Carefully, Andrea made her way through the maze of tables, ignoring the hat girl's request to check her coat. Andrea stopped at the booth. She looked down at Michael. He didn't look up, sitting hunched over the table. She bent down and gave him a long kiss. When she broke away from the embrace, she sat opposite him.

"Andrea, it's no good, despite our feelings for one another," he said.

Andrea giggled. Michael looked at her in surprise.

"This is serious," he said. "It just can't work, regardless of how much we love one another."

She reached over and took a hold of his hand. He was about to pull it back, but relented.

"Michael, it's alright. You are not my grandfather's child." she emphasized.

"What?" he said loudly.

Several people in the club glanced over at the booth. Michael put his hand to his mouth.

"What did you say?" he whispered, after the people went back to their eating and drinking.

Andrea smiled. "Yes. It's true. I just came from talking with Marty Fieldman and Mother. They confirmed you're not grandfather's child. You're my beautiful bastard," she snickered.

Andrea got up and slid into the side of the booth next to him. She wrapped her arms around him. Michael put his arm around her. She could see the relief in his expression.

"So now darling, we can get married without worrying about having three eyed children?" Andrea kidded.

Michael glanced at her with a concerned expression on his face. "Is Lizzy really my mother?" he asked.

"Yes," Andrea replied."

"Then who's my father. Andrea repositioned herself closer to Michael. "Lizzy said it was some hippie in the commune but he left after he found out she was pregnant."

Michael frowned. "Good lord, I'm really am a bastard."

The two were suddenly distracted by the head waiter standing next to the booth.

"Ahem . . ." the waiter uttered to get their attention.

They glanced up at him.

"Mr. Maxwell, please. You two will ruin the character of the club," he whispered.

Andrea straightened up and blushed. Michael adjusted his tie.

"Would you and Andrea like something, another drink Mr. Maxwell?"

"No thank you. We were getting ready to leave," Michael replied.

The waiter left. Michael took Andrea's hand.

"Come on. Let's get out of here so we can be alone."

Andrea got up and followed Michael. He got his coat from the hat check girl and put it on. The two walked out of the building. Andrea wrapped her arms around him. A valet, noticing Michael leaving the club, motioned for a car attendant to bring his car. When his car arrived, they got in.

"Where are we going?" Andrea asked.

"I don't know."

"Let's go to my place," she suggested.

Michael agreed. He wanted to be alone with her. He drove through the crowed streets. Little was said between them. Ten minutes passed when Michael stopped in front of Andrea's apartment building. They got out and Michael handed the keys to a car attendant. As they reached the entrance, the doorman greeted them.

"Good evening Mr. Maxwell. Miss Maxwell."

Michael acknowledged the greeting with a nod.

Andrea giggled as they stepped into the lobby.

"What's so funny?" Michael asked.

"Mr. Maxwell, Miss Maxwell," Andrea laughed, imitating the doorman. "That sounds so funny."

The couple walked to the elevator, both pushing a button to call one of the cars. Directly, one of the elevator doors opened. They stepped inside. When the door closed, they embraced and kissed passionately as the elevator ascended. They held the kiss, not aware that the elevator had reached her floor and the door had opened. An elderly couple was standing in front of the cab. The distinguished looking gentleman cleared his throat in an attempt to get their attention.

Startled by the sudden sound, they broke the embrace.

"It's okay," Michael said. "She my niece. Where getting married."

The two expressed shock at what Michael had said. Andrea giggled as they walked down the hall to her suite. She opened the door. Michael stepped inside her apartment, Andrea following. As she closed the door behind, she secured the latch.

The apartment was furnished with contemporary furnishings. An overstuffed brown leather sofa and chair faced a fireplace, accented by a deep pile beige carpet. The walls were adorned with copies of paintings by Rembrandt, Renoir and other masters. Embers in the fireplace were still glowing from a previous fire.

"Do you want me to make a drink?" Michael asked.

"Yes, darling," she answered, while walking over to the stereo. Picking up CD, she put it in the player. Instantly Frank Sinatra's voice filled the room.

Michael looked over at her from the bar. "Good choice."

Andrea pondered Michael a moment, watching as he prepared the drinks. Finished, he walked over to her and handed her a drink. She took a sip, and then set her glass down.

"I'm going to change into something more comfortable," she said. "Put another log on the fire darling, I'll just be a moment."

Michael walked over to the fireplace, picked up a log from the rack and placed it on the dwindling embers. He sat on the overstuffed chair in front of it, awaiting Andreas' return.

Several minutes passed and Andrea stepped into the living room. She took hold of her drink and walked to where Michael was sitting. She was wearing a short length silk robe revealing her shapely legs.

"Let's just sit by the fire for awhile," she suggested. She sat on a thick area rug placed on the carpet in front of the fireplace. Michael got up from the chair and sat down next to her.

Reaching up, she grabbed Michael's tie, pulling him to her. They both set their glasses on the fireplace stone ledge. Without saying anything, they embraced and kissed passionately.

"Michael, I want you now," she said.

Although Michael wanted to wait until their wedding night, in their passion, the two made love, forever sealing the bond between one another.

They stayed by the fire place savoring the perfect ending of a day that hadn't started out as such.

As the fire began to dwindle, Michael suggested they get something to eat.

While Michael was dressing, Andrea went into the bedroom and did the same. Michael walked into her bathroom and combed his hair while she finished putting on her make-up. He looked admiring at her reflection in the mirror.

He bent down and whispered in her ear. "I wanted to wait until we were married, remember?"

She giggled. "So we had any early honeymoon." Reaching up she tapped him on the nose. "Come on. Let's go."

"Where to?" he asked.

"We can eat at the club. Besides I left my car there."

They left the apartment and headed to the club. Andrea and Michael said little as they traveled to the club, savoring the pleasures they had just experienced. Andrea put her head against his shoulder. She was ebullient, as was Michael.

"Michael," she asked, "are you disappointed at me for enticing you? Giving up my virginity?"

He glanced at her. "No, darling. I'm happy we made the commitment. We are now one. No one can take that away from us."

Andrea smiled, snuggling closer to him. Little more was spoken as they continued onward.

Having reached the club, Andrea and Michael got out of the car and walked inside. The head waiter escorted the couple to a table. When seated, they each ordered drinks, then made selections from the menu.

"I'm so happy I could scream," Andrea said, suddenly.

Michael looked at her from across the table. The soft light radiating from the candle at the center of the table enhanced her beauty.

"Not here. We'll get thrown out."

Andrea smiled. "They wouldn't dare."

Michael was about to say something when the waiter came up to their table. He set the meals in front of them. The two sat enjoying their meals while making small talk. It was a perfect ending for a day that had not started out as such. Finished eating, they migrated to the bar for a few more drinks. Sated, and after a few night caps, they left the club. They kissed as each waited for their cars to be brought to them. Andrea and Michael parted, heading in their own directions to get some much needed rest.

CHAPTER SIXTEEN

IT SEEMED LIKE a few minutes after closing her eyes, when Andrea was suddenly awakened by the sunlight shining through her bedroom window, striking her face. She rolled over, pulling the covers over her head in an attempt get a little more sleep. It was to no avail, as her Persian cat began to play with the movement of her hand under the covers. She flipped the blanket off her.

"Oh, what's the use?" she said aloud. "May as well get up."

She jumped out of bed, put on her bathrobe and walked to the kitchen. She put some water in the coffee pot, grounds in the basket, and turned the pot on to perk. Finished in the kitchen, she went into the bathroom to dress and put on her makeup.

Emerging from the bathroom, ready for the new day, she walked to the kitchen and poured herself a cup of coffee. Sitting on a window bench, she looked outside and watched as children played in the city park across from her apartment building. The warm sunlight hit her face. She smiled, trying to visualize what her children might look like.

Although the previous day had ended happily, Andrea was aware of the unresolved issues that had to be settled. She wasn't sure what to do about her mother, or how she would react knowing that she had given herself to Michael before her wedding day. She pondered Andrew. She was saddened, knowing he had little time to live.

Andrea knew what she had to do. Even though he was her father, she did not feel the closeness that normally would be experienced between daughter and father. She made a promise that she would go see him in the hospital, although not sure of what she was going to say or how to act. She hoped it wouldn't be a tearful meeting.

Finished with the coffee, she got up and set the cup in the sink. Making sure everything in the apartment was secure, she walked out of her suite and made her way to her car and headed for the center.

Reaching the center, Andrea headed directly to her mother's office. Upon reaching the office, she knocked on the door.

"Come in," Claire called, from behind the closed door.

Andrea opened the door and stepped inside. She walked to the desk. Andrea could see Claire had been crying.

Andrea remembered her mother telling her it was best to sleep one night before making any drastic decisions or to come to unwarranted conclusions when involved in an emotional crisis. She was right.

Although it was difficult for Claire to look at her daughter, she reluctantly looked up at Andrea.

"Mother," she said. "I know what you tried to do for me. I appreciate all you've done, but you were wrong in keeping information about my father from me. I know about Marty and what he did. He's still my uncle. And my father? I know it's a hard pill to swallow, but the fact remains, he is still my father."

"I'm sorry, darling," Claire said. "I know what I did was wrong. All I can do is asking for your forgiveness."

What about Michael? You have no right feeling the way you do about him. I don't care who his parents are. I love him, and we will get married with or without your blessing. Besides, we made love last night. I'm no longer a virgin."

Claire's face flushed. She lowered her eyes.

"I know you love him, Andrea. You have my word I'll not interfere and will gladly except him as your husband."

Andrea was relieved. "Well then, if you really mean what you say, I'll forgive you. Besides, I can't go on bearing any grudges against you. I love you too much, regardless of what happened in the past."

Claire stood up and walked to Andrea. She hugged her. "Oh baby, I'm so sorry," she said.

Andrea and Claire stood in the office hugging one another. The two cried, joyful the conflict between them had ended. Claire broke away from the embrace.

"What about Andrew? What are we to do about him?" Claire asked.

"Go see him," Andrea replied. "He needs to know I'm his daughter."

"Yes, darling, but first, let me tell him about you. It would be best if he heard about you from me instead of you suddenly appearing. It might be traumatic otherwise."

Andrea thought over her suggestion.

"Yes," she said after a moment. "It was enough of a shock for him to see you after all these years."

"Good," Claire said. "Let me freshen up. I'll go directly to the hospital. You can follow after you've made your rounds."

"I'll meet up with you at the hospital." Andrea said, then turned and walked to the door. She opened it and disappeared among the people milling about the center.

Claire walked to the bathroom. She washed her face and began to reapply her make-up. She looked into the mirror.

"What will I say? How can I tell him about Andrea after all these years? What will he do?" she asked.

For the first time in her life, she was experiencing fear. She could not remember when the last time she felt so apprehensive.

Finishing refreshing herself, she left her office and got into her car. Twenty minutes later, Claire stopped her car in a spot reserved for visiting doctors. She got out and entered the hospital. She approached a desk manned by an elderly woman wearing a volunteer's badge.

"Good morning," Claire greeted, as she reached the desk. "I'm Doctor Claire Maxwell. I would like to know in what room Andrew Simpson has been placed."

The woman returned her greeting and picked up the patient roster from the desk. She scanned the paper with her finger, stopping at the name Andrew Simpson.

"He's in room 216," the elderly woman replied.

Claire thanked her and walked to the elevator lobby. She stepped into a waiting car and pressed the two button. Reaching the second floor, Claire stepped into the hallway. She scanned the numerous plagues along the corridor walls.

Noticing a sign which provided directions to the room she was looking for, she turned and continued on. She walked slowly, not sure of how she was going to explain Andrea to him.

"I should have taken a valium!" she said to herself.

Reaching the room, she was about to open the door when a nurse said. "Ma'am, visiting hours aren't until ten."

"I'm Doctor Maxwell. I'm attending to the patient in this room."

From the expression on her face, Claire realized the nurse may have a doubt as to her credentials.

Claire wasn't wearing the usual smock and trappings the nurse was accustomed to seeing.

Claire opened her purse and withdrew a badge indicating she was a visiting doctor of the hospital and attached it to her blouse.

"Excuse me, doctor," the nurse said, and quickly went about her daily routine.

Claire shrugged off the event, having experienced it several times in other hospitals.

Reaching the room Andrew was assigned to, Claire knocked on the door. There was no response. She knocked again. Still no response. Slowly, she opened the door, peering into the room. Looking down at the bed, to her surprise, it was empty.

She stepped into the room, letting the door close behind her. The bedding had been mussed, apparently by a one time occupant. She scanned the room, noticing a stand with an IV bottle hanging upside down with the usual plastic tube stringing down from it. The tube, terminating at a needle, laid on the bed, the fluid slowly seeping onto the bedding.

Her heart sank. She feared Andrew might have passed away before she could talk to him.

She was suddenly startled by a slight sound coming from behind a partially drawn curtain used to provide privacy for patients. Walking toward the foot of the bed, a cot came into view. She could see someone lying on it. Claire walked over to the cot. Looking down, she recognized Marty.

"What are you doing here?" she questioned.

Marty stirred from his sleep. He rolled over and looked up at Claire. Appearing surprised by her sudden appearance, he sat up in the cot. He waited a few seconds to get the sleep out of his eyes. When he was fully awake, he reached over and slipped on his pants.

"What brings you here?" he questioned, not realizing the bed Andrew had been resting in was vacated.

"Never mind me. What are you doing here?" she asked again.

Marty scratched at his head. "He took a turn for the worst last night. They called me, so I decided I had better come over and spend the night. It seems I'm the only one available. And you? I thought you didn't want to see him again?"

Claire could feel the chill in his voice.

"I came to tell him about Andrea."

Marty stood up. "It's about time."

"Did he pass away?"

"No. Not that I'm aware of," Marty replied. "I was supposed to be awakened if anything serious developed."

"Where is he?" Claire asked, looking at the empty bed.

Marty parted the curtain that had been blocking his view of the bed.

"I don't know."

Claire walked to the bed and pressed a button that rang a buzzer at the nurse's station.

Several minutes later the door opened. A nurse stepped in and looked around the room.

"Yes doctor? May I help you," she asked, glancing at Claire's badge.

"Where is the patient? Where is Mr. Simpson?"

The nurse looked at the empty bed. "Maybe he's in the bathroom."

The nurse knocked on the bathroom door. There was no reply. She opened the door. It was empty.

"I don't know where the patient is. I'll check with the nurse's station. Maybe the patient was taken down for some tests."

The nurse departed. Five minutes passed when she returned.

"I'm sorry, doctor. Mr. Simpson is nowhere to be found in the hospital."

Claire walked to the closet. She opened it and looked inside. "Where are his clothes," she asked the nurse.

The nurse shrugged her shoulders. Claire looked at Marty.

"Marty, you don't suppose he left the hospital?"

"I can't say," Marty replied.

Claire turned to the nurse. "Have security search this hospital. We must find this patient. He's a very ill man."

The nurse left immediately to have security carry out the task. Marty and Claire stood in the room.

Half an hour passed. There was a knock on the door. Andrea stepped in the room.

"Mother, how did he . . ." She stopped short on noticing Marty. She walked over to him and hugged him warmly. "Hello Uncle Marty."

Marty looked down at the floor. "Hello Andrea."

"You needn't worry. Everything is fine."

She was about to say something else, when the door opened. The nurse reentered the room.

"He left the hospital. I don't know how, but he's gone. After describing Mr. Simpson, a guard on duty early this morning thought he was a visitor. The guard said, he told him he wanted to visit with a patient. The guard informed him of the visiting hours and made him leave."

Andrea looked around at everyone in the room.

"What's happening? she asked.

"Andrew is missing," Claire answered. "He disappeared, left the room sometime this morning."

Andrea and Claire glanced at Marty. He was puzzled, putting his hands in the air, indicating he was just as much as a loss for an explanation for Andrew's disappearance as they were.

"Where could he have gone? We've got to find him. He shouldn't be out of the hospital," Claire said, her voice filled with anxiety.

"I honestly don't know Claire," Marty replied.

The small group stood in the room, trying desperately to think of where Andrew might have gone. Several minutes of silence ensued.

"Suppose I call the police. They might be able to locate him," Claire said.

"Yes, good idea. You call the police," Marty said. "I'll go back to the scrap yard. Maybe he'll show up there."

Marty quickly left the room. Claire turned toward Andrea. She was on the verge of tears, saddened by the disappearance of her father.

"We'll find him, darling," Claire said, trying to brighten her spirits. "Come with me. We can drive around the city and look for Andrew. With the two of us looking, we might have a better chance of seeing him."

Andrea managed a smile. "Yes. I'll come along," she said.

Claire and Andrea left the room. Claire stopped at the admissions desk when they reached the lobby. She called the police station, describing Andrew and informing them of his condition. She told them he could possibly die on the streets if not found in time. Finishing the conversation, she hung up the phone and motioned for Andrea to come with her.

The two left the hospital and made their way to Claire's car. Claire began driving aimlessly throughout the city in search of Andrew, not sure of where to look.

Marty drove into his scrap yard, parking his car next to the weigh shack. On seeing Marty, Shamus unlocked the side door and opened it for him.

"Didn't expect you back so early," Shamus said.

"It's Andrew," Marty replied. "He's disappeared from the hospital. I came back to see if he showed up here. Did he?"

"No, he hasn't showed up here, perhaps he will later. Do you want me to stay here or shall I go?" Shamus questioned.

"No," Marty replied. "Stay here and finish the day out. I might have to leave suddenly."

Marty paced the room, while drinking a cup of coffee. He was distraught, knowing Andrew could not last long, away from the hospital. Impatient, he returned to the rear of the room and placed the cup back on the shelf. Walking to the door, he opened it and stepped outside. As he reached the service window, he tapped on it. Shamus opened the window.

"I'm going to see if I can find Andrew. I'll be back later."

Shamus nodded and closed the service window as Marty continued toward his car. Marty quickly drove out of the scrap yard to search the streets. Knowing habits of alcoholics, he decided to search the various liquor stores throughout the city in the hopes that he would see Andrew or one of the many street people who frequented his scrap yard.

Although the sun was shining, the cold seemed to penetrate to the very marrow of his bones. Andrew walked slowly as the encrusted snow, glazed by the sun, gave way under his weight. He tightened his coat around him in an attempt to keep warm from the continuously dropping temperature. He labored at every step, breathing heavily, his breath disappeared like wisps of clouds being evaporated by the sun.

Although he had been free of pain while in the hospital, it slowly began to reappear. He stopped for a few minutes, as an intense stabbing pain ran through his body. The pain easing, he continued onward, slowly making his way through the city park.

People passed him going about their business, unaware of his plight. Andrew thought it was just as well, not wanting to be a burden on anyone. Coming to a bench, he sat down to rest as his energy dwindled with every step.

Reaching into his coat pocket, he withdrew the contents. To his amazement, he found thirty dollars.

Along with the money was a note. Carefully he unfolded the note and read it. It was from Marty.

"Here is a little spending money to carry you over until you get back to work."

Andrew put the money back into his pocket, reasoning that Marty had placed it in his coat pocket while in the hospital for the stab wound. He thought about Marty for a moment, searching his memory to see if he could recall having met him in the past, his mind reverting back to the sixties. Andrew vaguely remembered someone looking like him.

He visualized Marty without the scars, assuring himself he was the Martin he knew from the past. Once again Claire came to mind. Tears came to his eyes as he thought about her. He was embarrassed and ashamed about his present state and felt he could not face her again.

Rested, he stood and continued walking through the park. Stopping a few seconds, he watched a little girl at play in the snow while a woman looked on. The woman noticed Andrew watching. She went to the little girl, took her hand and quickly left the park. Andrew did not feel offended by the actions of the woman, having experienced such in the past. With increased difficulty, he continued walking, finally reaching the end of the park. As was his custom, he kept to the buildings as he made his way along the sidewalk. The multitude of people milling about hid Andrew from view of passing cars.

Tired by the walk, he finally made it to his destination. With difficulty, he stepped up to the vestibule of the liquor store he had frequented many times in the past. Opening the door, he went inside, letting the door close behind him. He stood a few minutes to enjoy the warmth. The clerk tending the counter looked up at him. He recognized Andrew. Without saying a word, the clerk reached up to a shelf and took down a bottle of wine. Andrew stopped him.

"No. Not wine. I'll have the whisky," he said, pointing to his selection as he walked up to the counter.

The clerk set the bottle back on the shelf and took the selected pint of whiskey off the shelf.

"Five," Andrew said, without hesitation.

The clerk looked at him. "Do you have the money to pay for this?" he asked.

Andrew nodded without replying.

The clerk took four more bottles from the shelf and set them on the counter alongside the first bottle. The clerk rang up the sale. "That'll be twenty seven fifty," he said.

Andrew reached into his pocket and withdrew the money and handed it to the clerk. Surprised, the clerk rang up the sale and handed Andrew his change. He was about to place the pint bottles in a paper bag when Andrew held up a hand.

"No bags," he instructed.

Andrew took the bottles and began to place each in a separate pocket of his coat. The clerk without saying anything watched him carefully. He suddenly grimaced as a sharp pain pierced him.

"Are you alright?" the clerk asked.

"Yeah, I'll be fine in a second. It's just a slight pain. It'll pass," Andrew replied.

The pain, once again easing, Andrew continued placing the bottle in the various pockets of his coat. Finished, he thanked the clerk and left the liquor store. The clerk shook his head as the door closed.

Andrew, wanting to be out of the public's view, headed for an alley. Reaching the alley and assured no one was watching, he quickly withdrew one of the pint bottles. With much difficulty and fumbling, he managed to remove the metal cap, the only obstacle in the way of his immediate desire. He put the bottle to his mouth and took several swigs. Instantly the whiskey began to warm him as it traveled down his throat. The false feeling of inner warmth he was accustomed to, returned.

Sitting down, he leaned against the building for support. He finished the first pint of whiskey in a matter of minutes. The pain he was experiencing began to subside to a dull ache, an ache he had come to know and was accustomed to. He was about to withdraw another pint, when he noticed someone walking into the alley. Standing up and about to continue his journey, someone called out his name. He waited, apprehensive, until the stranger came closer. It was Chancy.

Andrew looked at him in surprise. "You survived that auto accident and time in the poky," he said, smiling, knowing what Chancy had had to go through. "For a minute, I thought you were a goner when you stepped in front of that car."

Chancy laughed. "Just a slight brush, nothing serious, although they made me spend several days in the tank to dry out."

Andrew was glad to see Chancy. Throughout the years, the two had become friends in an odd way, one relying on the other.

Chancy eyed Andrew. "You got something? I'm out. Being locked up and all, I hadn't a chance to find enough scrap to earn me a bottle."

Andrew knew what Chancy meant. Knowing his time was near, Andrew reached into his pocket and withdrew the last of the money he had, the change given to him by the liquor store clerk. He handed the money to Chancy. Chancy took the money.

"Thanks Andrew," he said.

Chancy turned and started to walk away.

Andrew suddenly called out to him. "Chancy wait a minute!"

Chancy returned.

Andrew, reaching into one of his overcoat pockets, removed one of the pint bottles of whiskey. He handed the bottle to Chancy. Chancy's eye brightened at seeing the treasure.

"Thank you Andrew. Thanks a million," Chancy said gleefully as he put the bottle into his pocket.

"Chancy," Andrew said. "I haven't long to live. I'm dying. That's why I've given you that bottle and the money. You're a true friend. You take care of yourself. Maybe sometime we'll meet on the other side when you cross over, God willing."

Chancy gazed at him with a confused expression. "You don't mean that, do you?"

Andrew didn't answer his question. "You just get along. What's to happen to me will happen. I have no control over it. It's too late."

"I love you Andrew," Chancy said.

A tear came to Andrew eyes. "I love you too."

Chancy looked down at the pavement, pausing a few seconds. "Listen Andrew, I've gotta go," he said suddenly, evading his glance.

Andrew understood. "Get out of here," he said.

Concerned more about the prize whiskey in his pocket, Chancy turned around and quickly made his way out of the alley, waving at Andrew as he disappeared around the building.

Andrew watched as Chancy disappeared out of sight. "Good-bye friend," Andrew said quietly.

He got up and continued journeying the back streets and alleys. Relieved of the pain from the alcohol ingested, his pace quickened. He felt renewed, the alcohol giving him a false sense that nothing was wrong.

As he walked onward, clouds began appearing, hiding the sunshine. Normally a cold front coming into the city would bother him. Andrew ignored the sudden change, determined to make his way to his haven.

Unhindered, he finally made his way to his alley he called home. Traveling the depths, he stopped at its end. Looking around, he reached into the alcove and retrieved the cardboard he had previously tucked away. Placing the flatten box on the ground, he sat down.

Withdrawing another pint of whiskey, he opened the bottle and put it to his mouth. He took a long swig, half emptying the bottle. He attempted to ignore the pain that began to increase in intensity.

His mind began to wander. He thought of Andrea, Claire, and Martin.

"Oh lord, forgive me. I love them all," he said quietly.

Andrew carefully set down the bottle as his vision began to blur. He held his hand on the bottle for a moment, balancing it to keep it from tipping over. Gradually his hand relaxed its grip. The bottle tipped over, the liquid he held precious spilled onto the ground. With a sigh, he became unconscious.

Marty drove the streets endlessly, going from liquor store to liquor store in an attempt to locate Andrew. His efforts were in vain.

Driving down Fifth Street, Marty suddenly notice Chancy going into a liquor store, he stopped his car got out and entered the store. Inside, he watched as Chancy made his purchase. The clerk looked up at Marty.

Marty walked up to Chancy.

"Excuse me. Do you know Andrew?" Marty asked.

Chancy was cautious, confirming, "I know an Andrew. Why?"

"I need to know where he is," Marty replied. "He's very sick and needs to be in a hospital."

Chancy looked at Marty with suspicion. "He's probably back in his alley," Chancy said.

"His alley?" Marty questioned.

"Yeah, it's on Third, between the night club and restaurant."

Marty turned and as quickly as he could, exited the liquor store, got into his car and drove off. As he made his way through the streets, he passed Claire going in the opposite direction. Marty honked his horn to get her attention. Claire motioned, indicating she was aware of his presence. Marty pulled over to the curb and waited until Claire pulled up behind him. Claire stopped behind Marty's car. He got out and walked to Claire. She rolled down the window as he approached her. The snow began to fall with such fury it instantly covered anything it rested upon.

"Third, an alley next to the night club," Marty said. "He might be there."

Claire put her car in gear and began driving in the direction Marty had indicated. Marty quickly got into his car and followed close behind Claire.

The two cars stopped halfway down the alley. Claire and Andrea got out of the car and waited until Marty joined them.

The mood was solemn. The three looked at one another without saying anything. They each feared what they would find. In anticipation, they walked down the alley towards its end. They could see the slumped body of Andrew prostrate on the ground, motionless.

"Oh no! He can't be gone," Andrea said, the tears beginning to stream down her face.

Claire could not contain herself. Despite her cold nature, she likewise began to cry.

Marty, as quickly as he could, made his way to where Andrew was laying. Claire and Andrea stood fast. Marty reached down and shook Andrew in an attempt to rouse him. There was no immediate response. Marty turned, looking in the direction of Claire and Andrea. He shook his head, saddened, sure the end had finally come for Andrew. The cold November wind traveled down the alley, decaying among the lifeless body of Andrew. The snow, every increasing, covered the motionless body lying on the ground.

Marty was about to walk away from Andrew, when suddenly Andrew whispered. "Martin."

Marty turned around. He quickly walked up to him and knelt down beside him.

"Andrew, I'm here. So is Claire and Andrea," Marty whispered.

Andrew looked up at Marty. His expression was one of being at peace. "I know. Bring them to me," he said his voice barely audible.

Marty quickly motioned for Claire and Andrea to come near.

The two walked to where Andrew was laying. They looked down at him. He motioned for Claire to approach. Claire knelt down.

"Andrew," she said, "forgive me."

Andrew managed a smile. "Don't worry about it. I forgave you a long time ago. Now let me see Andrea."

Claire motioned for Andrea to come nearer. She knelt down.

Andrew looked up at her and smiled. "You're so beautiful," he whispered, "the daughter I imagined you would be."

He sighed, and then exhaled his last breath.